I Hear You

Casey Morales

Casey Morales

Chapter 1

TYLER

I wheeled myself from beneath the Cadillac, sat up, and stretched my back. Every muscle in my body was knotted and aching. I glanced down to find my normally spotless shirt was more dingy black than cloudless blue. Nothing had been easy with today's patient, and my uniform had taken the brunt of its defiance.

"You look like shit, pretty boy," a familiar voice said. Sam Prescott never missed the chance to give me grief.

"Don't take this the wrong way, boss, but you're no rose yourself."

"Ha. I'm smokin' hot, and you know it. It's a wonder you've kept your hands off me this long."

"Yeah, a total wonder," I deadpanned as I struggled to my feet. Sam had been my best friend from the first day I started working for him. He was rough around the edges, but a great guy. "God, my back is stiff. This car's a beast. Can we just shoot it?"

"I'm not sure bullet holes are what we're paid for." Sam's grin widened. "Is she done? I promised the owner a call today before we closed, and it's seven thirty."

"Yeah, just need to have one of the guys clean her up."

"Right, first thing in the morning. Let's get out of here." He turned, then called back over his shoulder. "Any Friday night plans?"

"Nah. I'm beat. May just watch a little TV and hit the sack early."

"Wow. Nashville's most prominent party boy passing up a Friday night? Is that even allowed? Please tell me you haven't screwed your way through the entire phone book already."

I flicked him the bird, and he laughed.

"Hey, even us pros need a break. It takes a lot of energy to please this town's A list. Besides, tomorrow's supposed to be a big night at Shadow Box. There's been rumors about some high-end DJ and a guest performer on the agenda. It's got all the boys worked up, and I want to be in my best form. You know I can't leave with anything less than best in show, right?"

"Sweet Jesus, no. That would be a serious party foul, probably get splattered all over the front cover of the *Nashville Scene*. I can see the headline now: Gay World Rocked as Nashville's Most Eligible Bachelor Leaves Bar with a Nine. How would you live with yourself?"

"I do have a rep to maintain." I winked, then braced myself against the Caddie and rose. "What about you guys? Ever gonna leave your cave and let us boys admire your domestic bliss?"

Sam rolled his eyes. "Yeah, we're pretty domestic. Miguel will probably have dinner on the table when I walk in."

"Aww, such a good little gay. You already have him trained. Does he wear an apron too?"

Sam grabbed a rag and tossed it at me. "You should see when he cooks with nothin' but the apron—"

"Alright. Enough. I don't need to hear about your disgustingly happy life."

Sam beamed. Mr. Rough-and-tumble was truly whipped. "You should try it. There's something to be said for knowing what you're walking into each night."

"I know exactly what's waiting for me at home. Dom's always happy to see me."

Domino was my one-year-old border collie. A neighbor back home in Pensacola was a breeder and gave him to me as a birthday present. He was barely bigger than both my hands together when I held him that first time. I hadn't really wanted a dog, or the responsibility that came with having a child, but now I couldn't imagine life without him. Unfortunately, as smart as he was proving to be, he had yet to learn to cook dinner. Sam had me beat on that score.

He shook his head, then vanished into his office.

I held my hands under a stream of scalding water for a long moment before lathering up in a sad attempt to wash off the Cadillac's residue.

It was eight o'clock by the time I climbed into my old Ford pickup and pulled out of the lot. The road blurred in my vision, and the full weight of the day settled firmly about my shoulders. Tired didn't begin to describe how I felt, but I knew Dom would be excited and need to burn off energy the moment I crossed my apartment's threshold. I turned into the parking lot of Buddy Brew, a local coffee shop a couple blocks from my house. I'd never keep up with the little beast, but I had to at least stay awake while walking him.

The coffee shop's parking lot was packed, but when I entered, the only sounds that greeted me were the chatter of baristas and the whirring of grinders. The comforting smell of burnt beans and cinnamon tickled my nose.

I glanced around the shop to find a group of guys in the far corner sitting in a wide circle of pulled-together chairs. They listened intently as one spoke in low tones I couldn't make out. A table near the window was occupied by a man with a laptop. Several long-dead paper cups and a plate containing the mutilated remains of a muffin lay scattered about his computer. The poor guy was probably a writer or student and had sat there for hours staring at a blinking cursor. I couldn't imagine a slower way to die.

A young woman in a Belmont University T-shirt sat with her legs curled beneath her in a puffy chair. She eyed me a couple times, and I flashed her my best *I see you checking me out* smile. She shook her head, then pointed at my chest. I glanced down to find a large swath of grease I'd missed when cleaning up. How it got past the powder-blue bowling shirt every tech at the shop wore was a wonder. AC/DC would never forgive me for smearing car guts all over a vintage shirt bearing their logo.

"Damn it," I muttered as I wiped the oily smear with a napkin, only succeeding in spreading it further across and into the fabric. The girl grinned at my distress then returned her attention to her book.

I sighed and leaned against the counter, resigned to a day that had beaten me senseless.

"Poor thing. You look so sad." Woody, the surfer-dude-turned-barista, nearly startled me out of my shirt. "Want your usual, big guy?"

"Hey, Woody, sure. Can you add an extra shot though? I'm dead on my feet tonight."

"Sure thing, dude. One large mocha latte, no whip, room for skinny cream, add choco shavings, a shot of hazelnut, and an extra shot—in an extra-large cup—coming right up."

"When you say it like that, I sound pretty high maintenance."

"If the slipper fits, Dorothy." He cocked a brow, then turned to make my decidedly *not* high-maintenance drink, chuckling all the way.

I drifted to the end of the counter where my caffeine boost would be delivered and aimlessly perused the new mugs they had on offer. One was molded like a grinning bear's face, complete with teeth whose tips dripped coffee. Another bore the image of the shop's founder, Buddy Adams, now an octogenarian who rarely set foot in the place. His broad smile and thinning white hair made the chocolate-colored mug pleasant enough, but it still felt a little weird.

A sudden burst of laughter pulled my head up. The guys in the circle were all teeth and gums. Some clapped, while others laughed and waved jazz hands in the air. Their amusement was infectious, but there was something different in the tones of their laughter. Curiosity drew me into their world.

They were an odd mix of ages, especially for Buddy Brew, who usually catered to the twenty-something and college crowd. Half the men looked to be in their thirties or older. The speaker and a few who sat around him were close to my own age of twenty-nine. One lone youngster giggled on the far side of the circle, appearing no more than sixteen or seventeen. The little puddin' wore a T-shirt small enough for a preteen girl, which had more sequins than a Hollywood actress at the Oscars. Thick, flamingo-pink eyeliner completed his look.

Most in the group wore some kind of hearing aid—and not the tiny kind designed to disappear. These were large, flesh-colored hunks of plastic, and some were attached to thumb-sized microphones that hung about their neck. When the kid's fingers started flying, it all clicked into place.

"One chocolate death, good sir." I turned to find Woody extending a cup across the counter. He followed my gaze and nodded. "They're here most Fridays. Fun guys."

I grabbed my drink and turned back toward the group as they settled and focused on the speaker again.

"They're all deaf?" I asked.

"Yeah. It's the local gay deaf group. I forget what they call themselves. It's a play on the flag and an ear. Rainbow Lobes? Canals? No . . . drums. That's it. Rainbow Drums. Or is it Drumettes? I can't ever remember."

I chuckled. "That's a really terrible group name. They know that, right?"

"I don't know. Seems to fit, I guess. Pretty cool they can make fun of themselves like that."

I hadn't meant to stare, but I couldn't pull my eyes away. One of the guys seated beside the speaker caught me looking and returned my gaze. I wasn't sure if he was annoyed I'd in-truded into their personal space or, I don't know, found my greasy shirt attractive?

Yeah, he looked annoyed.

He ran a hand through a mess of wavy brown hair and glanced away, then back up at me.

"Holy cow, those eyes," I muttered.

The guy flashed a grin, then returned his attention to the group.

The warmth of the coffee in my hand somehow traveled up my arm and into my chest.

Shit, he was cute.

Woody chuckled. "Uh-huh. That's Gabe. He's freakin' adorable. Careful though. That pack is protective."

Pack? Protective?

"Thanks for the java." I gave Woody a coffee cup salute and made my way toward the exit.

As I turned and pressed my back into the glass door, another burst of laughter broke the shop's silence. I looked up to find Gabe staring at me again. His eyes sparkled, and his smile was warm as he laughed at some private jest. I couldn't help grinning back and raising my cup toward him. I guess he hadn't expected that, because his eyes widened and one hand raised in a tentative wave as I pushed my way out into the night.

Chapter 2

GABE

A sharp elbow found its way into my side, and I turned to find a shit-eating grin splayed across Bryan's face.

"Who was that?" he mouthed. His eyes darted to the coffee shop's door then back to me.

I shrugged. Bryan still struggled with lipreading, so I signed, "Don't know."

"He was hot and totally into you," his fingers flashed back.

"I don't even know who he is. Let's just listen to Lucas, okay?" I hoped invoking our senior guncle would distract my young friend. He was like a golden retriever that way. Anything shiny or muscular completely derailed any thought he might've held a moment earlier.

In that moment, the golden had a bone clenched between its sharp teeth and wasn't about to let go. His elbow jabbed again.

"You should find out. I bet Woody knows."

"I'm not a stalker, Bry."

He grinned. "I am. Wait here."

I tried to grab his leash . . . I mean, arm . . . but he was too quick. The little shit bounded to his feet and out of our chair circle faster than I could move. I tried not to watch too closely as he struggled to chat with our favorite barista, then flitted his way to land back in his seat.

"His name is Tyler. He's a mechanic, and he's single. You're welcome." He crossed his legs and batted his eyelashes dramatically.

A hand on my other arm nearly spun me around.

"You two paying attention?" Lucas asked. His gestures were sharp, annoyed, almost as much as his eyes.

"Sorry, Papa," I signed, and lowered my eyes in mock submission.

He gestured a downturned *okay* sign: "Asshole."

"Hey!"

He did a Groucho brow raise, grinned, then turned back to the group and resumed whatever joke he'd been telling before our banter had stolen his mojo.

At thirty-nine, Lucas was an old man. He could be cranky and crusty, and his stubborn, stick-in-the-mud mindset drove me nuts, but I knew it belied the biggest heart in Nashville. Everyone in the circle admired him. No, that's an understatement. We all loved him with a fierceness most would never understand.

"Hello? Gabriel?" Lucas said as he waved his hand in front of my face.

My eyes snapped up. "Sorry. Guess I was daydreaming." I glanced around to find the group standing and dispersing. I couldn't believe I'd been that lost in thought.

Bryan wedged his way between us. "He's in love."

The little shit.

"I am not." I stabbed my thumb across my chin enough to punch him playfully in the chest.

"What's this? Gabe's in love? Do tell."

Shit, now Lucas was in the boat.

"I'm *not* in love. I saw a cute guy, and he smiled at me. That's all. I don't even know who he is."

"Yes, you do." Bryan grabbed my elbow and pulled me to my feet, then signed, "I got his name, occupation, and a mule to pass messages."

"Pass messages? What am I, twelve?"

"Sometimes I wonder," he said, triumphant I served him a soft ball.

Lucas leaned in to get my attention, then signed, "You talking about that hot guy with grease all over him?"

"Yes. His name's Tyler," Bryan offered, before I could deny any knowledge of the man.

Lucas scowled. "Do we need to have the talk about dating hearing men again?"

I rolled my eyes. "Please, no. I haven't even met him. There's no need for the Holy Talk, Uncle Luc."

He eyed me a moment, then nodded. "Good. Gotta keep my boys happy and healthy. You know that."

His boys.

Lucas was something else—and very serious about protecting *his* boys.

Bryan's attention span had reached its gnat's-length limit. He grabbed my arm again and pulled me to the exit. "I'm leaving. Gabe, talk to Woody. Please."

I smiled. Bryan was twenty-two, but looked fifteen. When he got excited, his overly dramatic toothy grin lit up the room.

"I'll think about it, okay?"

"Good." He gave me a peck on the cheek and flew the coop. It was all I could do to get through the door before it slammed in my face.

By the time I walked into my apartment, it was ten o'clock. Poor Audie had been cooped up for hours, and nearly bowled me over when I walked through the doorway. I dropped to the hardwood and let her lick until I was soaked.

"I love you too, baby girl," I said between laps of her tongue.

Audie was a two-year-old, hundred-pound German shepherd who had more strength and speed than good sense. When she adopted me, she was only four weeks old, a bit too young to be separated from her mother. I had to bottle-feed her for weeks. Something in that simple act bonded us in ways I'd never experienced with a dog. Add to that I rarely went anywhere without her. She came to the academy with me every day, and was a huge help in training the more challenging dogs. The few hours each week when I ran errands or went to our group meetings were the only times we were apart—and she acted like I'd left her for a world tour every time.

As we strolled down the sidewalk on our last walk of the day, she dutifully sniffed every blade of grass or stray leaf we passed. The night was cool and clear, and only a few cars passed down our quiet street.

My mind wandered from my pup's playful diligence to the guy I'd seen earlier in the coffee shop. He *was* cute. No, he was hot. Some might be turned off by the dingy muck smeared across his T-shirt, but that made him sexier in my eyes. It didn't hurt that the shirt was a tad small and showed off his muscular frame. The sleeves strained to contain arms with veins that looked more like a highway map. I wasn't usually into gym-worshipping meatheads, but something about his taut frame had made my heart skip a beat.

I tried to shake his image from my mind's eye, but it rebelled and panned up to his face. His dark hair stretched tight across his forehead to be bound by a band in the back, but a few locks had freed themselves and dangled across his face. I'd wanted to reach across the shop and push them back.

And his eyes. My god, those emeralds glittered with such intensity. I couldn't remember the last time I'd seen eyes that green.

Then he smiled before pushing through the doorway and—

Audie nipped at my hand to get my attention. I glanced down to find a mountainous pile of poop in the grass by the sidewalk. As I knelt to bag her little present, Audie wedged her nose under my armpit so it stuck through to my chin. I grinned and kissed her muzzle, then enjoyed a moment of unrelenting love flowing through her eyes. If I could bottle and sell the adoration in her gaze, I'd be a wealthy man.

Her ears suddenly perked up, and her head snapped toward the opposite side of the street where a middle-aged couple passed. I recognized them from our complex, but couldn't remember their names. They released each other's hand and waved. It was too dark for me to tell whatever they said, so I just waved back and watched as they reclasped hands and continued on their stroll. One of the guys laid his head on the other's shoulder for a second as they walked, in a simple, intimate gesture. It was a beautiful moment.

Audie nipped my hand.

"Alright, let's go home." She was already pointed in that direction at full leash length.

As we started home, I glanced back at the couple, and something in me stirred. I'd been alone when I arrived from Italy, but everything was fresh and new then, and Lucas had made sure I was embraced by his gaggle of gays. There hadn't been much time to feel that aloneness. Besides, I was a strong, independent guy. Despite all the challenges life tossed my way, I'd left my family and moved across the world, started my own business, and was building a successful life. Audie was my constant companion, and my circle of humans were more like family than friends.

So why did the sight of those two guys, who were clearly happy and in love, make me feel so lonely?

Chapter 3

TYLER

For nearly a year, my alarm clock had been little more than a paperweight.

At precisely six fifteen every morning, without fail, a blur of black and white shifts from the end of the bed to rest atop my chest. If I dare remain still, a pant ensues, bathing my face in warm, often noxious breath. Domino, my soon-to-be one-year-old border collie, is diligent in his daily routine, and, while humans might take weekends off to rest and relax, Dom's desire to work never abated.

I turned my head to avoid the insistent lick of his smooth, moist tongue. Dom leaned over and nuzzled his nose between my chin and the pillow, lifting my head back toward him so his tongue could continue raising the dead.

"Dom, buddy, Daddy's sleepy."

My voice activated the jumping bean in his brain, and the press of his weight transformed into a series of paw punches.

"Alright, fine. I'm getting up."

He did a full spin on the bed, then leapt off and gave me a sharp bark that translated into, "Yay, Daddy, it's morning. I'm hungry. Let's play. Can we eat and play? Daddy? Can we? Daddy?"

What parent doesn't recognize *that* gleam in their child's eyes?

He sat dutifully before me and glared as I heaved myself up for my morning duties. The moment my bearing shifted, he was off, bounding into the kitchen.

A familiar mechanical voice echoed down the hall. "Domino. Eat."

When I didn't move quickly enough, I heard, "Domino. Eat. Domino. Eat. Eat. Eat."

"I'm coming. Jesus, can't a guy pee in peace?"

"Domino. Eat. Daddy. Eat."

Why had I ever bought those stupid buttons?

A few months ago, I'd run across YouTube videos on dog training. Dom was around eight months old, and I figured it was time to start educating the beast. As I scrolled through videos, I stumbled across a woman who'd used buttons to train her dog to communicate. Each button resembled the Easy Button sold at Staples, but was recordable so a dog's human could dictate specific words in his or her own voice. The dog in the video had fifty-seven buttons arrayed in a massive semi-circle on the floor. It was dizzying to watch the human remember which button was which. The dog never faltered.

When one video showed the dog press "Help. Sam. Hurt," I was captivated.

The owner asked, "Sam, where are you hurt?"

The dog immediately pressed a button that said, "Paw."

Sure enough, the owner checked, and a burr was stuck in the dog's front right paw. I had to rewatch that video three times to believe it was real.

After that, Amazon couldn't deliver fast enough. Dom was the smartest dog I'd ever known. I was sure he could pick up on button training. His name and "Eat" were the first two buttons I bought.

Six weeks after I started pressing "Domino. Eat" before every meal, something clicked in his brain. I woke that morning to those two mechanical words followed by a proud pounce as he danced on my still-blanketed body. After a round of enthusiastic hugs and licks, he abandoned me, raced back to the kitchen, and pressed "Eat" another dozen times until I rose and followed his command.

He would turn one in three weeks, and there were already six buttons glued to a board beside the front door: Domino, Daddy, Eat, Love You, Play, and Park.

Midway through a bowl of Honey Nut Cheerios, the day began in earnest with, "Domino. Park. Play. Park."

I glanced across the kitchen to find the little shit sitting patiently by the front door with his leash between his teeth. His tail swished against the hardwood when his eyes met mine. I laughed through sugary milk.

"Okay, buddy. We'll go. Just let me finish my cereal."

The swishing intensified.

Dom danced in the passenger's seat, his tail a blur as he took in the sights and twirled in anticipation. Centennial Park was packed. The wide grassy areas that stretched from the main street to the steps of the Parthenon were dotted with couples on blankets and children running and playing. The sun shone brightly and a light breeze heralded the first hints of fall.

I loved this place.

Originally part of a larger farm owned by John Cockrill and his wife, Anne, the sister of one of Nashville's founders, the land had been used as a horse track, the state's fair grounds, and a public park.

In 1897, when Tennessee celebrated her centennial as a state, the site's name was changed to Centennial Park. Nashville's concentration of colleges and universities earned her the nickname "The Athens of the South," so, in honor of the occasion, a full-size replica of the Greek Parthenon was constructed. It was the centerpiece of the Tennessee Centennial and International Exposition, a temporary temple made of wood and plaster. The graceful building was so beloved that, following the celebration, private funds were raised to construct a permanent version on the site out of marble, reinforced steel, and concrete.

I pulled into a parking spot just beyond the massive bronze doors. Dom barely let me snap his leash on before leaping out of the car and tangling my legs in the line.

"Easy, buddy. I'm coming."

I grabbed his favorite ball from the floorboard, and the leash tightened further as his excited whimpers grew. I glanced back and raised a brow. His butt hit the pavement, and his eyes snapped to mine.

"Good boy." It amazed me how he could read my expressions and know exactly what I wanted. He was too smart for his own good.

We jogged around the walking trail a moment to burn off a little of his eager energy, then made our way to one of the large grassy fields that stretched before Athena's temple. Signs posted about the park insisted owners keep dogs leashed, but the working breeds were rarely tethered. A few others picnicked or strolled with their humans about the field, but nothing shook Dom's concentration when his ball was in my hand. The moment I unclipped him, he raced about me in tight circles and barked. I extended my hand, palm down, and he slammed his butt to the ground again. His tail was a blur of excitement. I couldn't hold back a deep laugh as I watched his eyes quiver.

"Go!" I called as I tossed his ball into the open field. A streak of black and white flew before me, returning seconds later to resume his ready pose. This went on for twenty minutes, and, while I made him stop and drink a few times, he never tired.

He'd pass out in the car on the way home, but while we remained at the park, his battery would never lose power.

The cheerful music of an ice cream truck sent children from all corners scurrying our way. Dom loved kids, but I knelt to clip on his leash anyway, just to put the parents at ease.

"He's cute," someone said behind me.

"Thanks. He knows it too," I said, scratching Dom's ear without turning around or looking up.

Whoever had spoken didn't respond, so I glanced back.

It was the guy from the coffee shop, the one with the wavy hair and cute smile.

"Uh, hey. Hi," I stammered.

Dom zipped around me, tangling my feet again. I lost my balance and tumbled backward onto the grass. The leash flew out of my hand and Dom darted toward the guy. By the time I managed to sit upright, the guy had both arms wrapped around my pup and was getting a full-face tongue bath. His lips were pressed into a tight line, but curled upward. I could swear his eyes were laughing.

"I'm so sorry." I climbed to my feet and grabbed the leash. "Dom, down. Here."

Dom immediately dropped and returned to my side.

The guy laughed and looked up, then quirked his brow at Dom. "He's amazing. Do you train him?"

Three things struck me in that moment. First, his voice was odd, like he had marbles in his cheek and was trying to speak through them. Second, his eyes gripped mine as he spoke. I'd met plenty of folks who maintained solid eye contact, but this guy's eyes were like lasers. It was a little unnerving. And third, the dimples that formed when he smiled made my insides squirm. He was beyond cute; he was freakin' adorable, just like Woody had said.

Suddenly a grade-school girl, my eyes dropped to Dom as I spoke. "Yeah, he's a good boy. I do what I can, but he picks up a lot on his own."

The gentle press of fingers lifting my chin nearly startled the leash out of my hand again. When our eyes met, the guy said, "I'm deaf. I need to see your lips to read them."

I nodded, then spoke with exaggerated slowness and heightened volume. "Oh, okay. Sorry."

He chuckled. "It doesn't matter how loud you talk, I still won't hear you."

My cheeks colored. I was such a dumbass. "I'm sorry. Of course ... I mean ... I'm an idiot. Jesus."

He laughed again, and my chest blazed at the brightness of his smile.

"I'm Gabe." As he introduced himself, he made a motion with his right hand.

I cocked my head.

He held his hand up with his index finger pointing toward me and his thumb raised, like the hammer of a little gun. He fired the gun a couple times, then turned it sideways and pressed his thumb to his forefinger. "That's a G." Then he patted the *G* against his heart a couple times. "That's how you sign my name, Gabe."

"A *G* over your heart?" I asked.

He nodded. "My mom said I was a lover not a fighter, so she made that sign for me. I'm not sure how a ten-year-old can be a fighter, but I like it anyway."

Without thinking, I asked, "Is your mom deaf?"

He shook his head. "I'm the only one."

"Were you born deaf?"

He shook his head again.

"I'm sorry. God, that's all so personal. Again, I'm an idiot. I shouldn't—"

"It's okay. Everybody asks. I'm used to it."

My head drooped, but he lifted it again. His touch sent a shiver through me. Dom sensed it and pressed himself against my leg, glaring up at me.

"You never told me your name," he said.

"Oh, sorry. I'm Tyler. This is Dom."

Gabe dropped to his knees and let Dom slobber on him again.

"He'll do that all day if you let him," I said.

Gabe didn't acknowledge my statement, and I realized his eyes were on Dom.

"He's great," Gabe said, looking back up at me as Dom's tongue attacked his neck.

"He likes everybody, but damn, I think he wants to keep you."

Gabe's mouth twisted, and his eyes sparkled.

"Uh . . . I mean . . . he . . . um. Never mind. I'm still an idiot. Want some ice cream?"

A confused look crossed Gabe's face, so I pointed behind him to the truck slowly creeping around the drive. Again, I'd forgotten he couldn't hear the siren song of the ice cream god as it rolled through the park.

His head wheeled around, then back to me. "Sure," he said.

"You okay to watch Dom? I'll go get it."

"Sure. I can handle this beast. A Tweety Bar, please."

God, could he get any cuter?

"One Tweety Bar, coming right up."

He turned back to Dom and gave him a hand signal. It took a second, then recognition dawned and Dom's butt hit the ground. A few seconds later, he was laying before Gabe, then rolling over. I could barely believe what I was seeing. Dom was a smart dog, smartest I'd ever known, but I hadn't taught him to roll over. Gabe barely spent five minutes with him and already he was following his every command. Then Gabe dropped to his knees and began wrestling with him on the ground. Laughter was punctuated by contented barks and playful growls. I watched a moment, then turned to retrieve our treats.

When I returned with ice cream in each hand, I found Gabe sitting with his legs crossed and Dom's head resting peacefully in his lap. My dog's eyes were closed.

What the hell? In the park?

"Is he *asleep?*"

My jaw must've dropped because Gabe grinned as he took his Tweety Bird on a stick from my hand. Dom's eyes popped open and followed the movement, but his head didn't budge.

Gabe licked his cartoon pop and shrugged. "I'm good with dogs."

"Yeah, I'd say so."

I dropped beside him and crossed my legs, then took a bite of my chocolate–dipped vanilla cone.

"God, I haven't had one of these in years." My eyes rolled back in ecstasy.

Gabe giggled. It was a throaty sound filled with childlike joy. His eyes were bright, and his smile was wide and unhindered. I couldn't remember the last time I'd seen someone so happy and . . I don't know . . . *free*. It reminded me of how I felt when I rode my bike. There was nothing like the sensation of soaring through the countryside.

"Woody said you go to Buddy Brew all the time," he said between licks. "I've never seen you there."

"I usually swing by in the morning on my way to work. I'm not a great morning person, especially without a jolt of java."

Dom lifted his head and sniffed at Gabe's ice cream. Rather than act annoyed, Gabe bent his head and rubbed his forehead against Dom's furry noggin, earning a round of affectionate licks that made Gabe giggle again. That warmth tickled my skin once more, then I realized he probably didn't even know how he sounded.

I felt like such a dumbass for thinking that, and couldn't decide whether I felt more guilty or stupid for letting my mind go there.

Gabe peered over Dom. "You want to ask about being deaf?"

My mouth opened, but nothing came out. *How the fuck did he know what I was thinking?*

"You've never known a deaf person, have you?"

I shook my head, then remembered to close my mouth.

"You don't have to dance around it. I'm not ashamed or anything. It's not who I am, but it is part of me, I guess. Ask whatever you want, okay?"

I nodded like it all made sense. It didn't.

I couldn't scrub the guilt or sadness—or whatever that pang was in my chest—at the thought of this sweet man not being able to hear. I took Dom's barks for granted. Hell, half the time they annoyed the shit out of me, but I couldn't imagine a day without hearing them. They woke me each morning, and his steady breathing soothed me to sleep at night. Across the park, two toddlers giggled and squealed as they ran. It was the most beautiful sound, and another Gabe would never hear or fully comprehend. I didn't even know this guy, and my heart was in my throat thinking about all the things he'd never hear.

Somehow, his nonchalance made the pang worse. He'd even made light of his disability.

Disability.

I heard myself say that word in my mind. Was it the right thing to call it? Would it be insulting or insensitive? I had no idea what words to use—or not use. Was struggling with all this its own form of insult? I wanted to say the right thing—to say anything to make him smile and laugh.

My mind spun, having no idea where to start.

It was all so . . . unfair.

"It's not unfair, if that's what you're thinking."

Shit, he was in my head again.

He laughed. "Yes, I am psychic. All deaf people are—but it's a secret. You can't tell anyone."

I gaped.

His laughter grew. "I'm just fucking with you."

My mouth made an O as I tried to catch up to the game he'd just played on me. Even Dom looked amused at my distress. The little traitor reached up and licked Gabe's chin, eliciting another boyish giggle.

Before either of us could recover, a thirty-something guy I remembered had been sitting next to Gabe at the coffee shop stepped in between us. He didn't look at me, just squared his shoulders to Gabe's and started signing so fast I thought his fingers might fly off. His brows were knitted together, and there was fire in his eyes. Gabe watched a moment, then began signing in return. I watched in amazement as they signed at the same time, clearly understanding everything each other was saying.

I couldn't even talk and listen at the same time.

As their conversation continued, Gabe's face lost its humor, and his gestures became sharp jabs. After a moment, the other guy grabbed his arm and pulled him upright.

"I'm sorry. I need to go. Thanks for the ice cream." Gabe handed Dom's leash to me as they turned to walk away. He glanced back over his shoulder and called out, "Don't forget to keep our secret. I'll know if you tell."

He winked and smiled one last time before his friend dragged him off the grassy field.

Dom whimpered and licked my hand.

I glanced down to find him staring after Gabe with his ears back and tail drooping.

Chapter 4

TYLER

Saturday afternoon, I took Dom for a run around the neighborhood. Summer had finally surrendered to fall, and the air held pleasant warmth with a hint of cooler days to come. By the time my foot struck the steps to my condo, I was coated in sweat. Dom was huffing, but looked like he could've run for another hour.

"If I had half your energy—"

He barked, as if taunting me over the phrase he'd heard since he was a pup.

"Come on, buddy, let's get something to eat."

As soon as I opened the door and unhooked his leash, he bolted into the condo and his button cried out from the kitchen: "Eat. Eat. Eat. Daddy. Eat."

I'd created a monster.

At eleven thirty, Dom pretended to sleep. In reality, his eyes opened into tiny slits when he thought I wasn't watching. Big Brother had nothing on a dog with a mission.

I smoothed by black T-shirt, ran my hand through my hair, and squirted cologne in all the right places. A quick mirror check confirmed I'd transformed from greasy mechanic to hot-as-fuck, ready-to-rumble, going-out gay boy. I winked at myself in the mirror, then laughed at my own stupidity.

There was a line to get into the Shadow Box that wound around the building from the parking lot. I strode by guys in tight jeans and tighter shirts, receiving an appreciative eye-lick from each guy I passed. The "walk of fame," as Sam called it, was one of my favorite parts of going out. The attention was fun, but I'd get that just by walking into the room. It was the curiosity factor that made me love it. The guys in line, at least those new enough to not already know who I was, drove themselves mad trying to guess why I could walk past the queue and be ushered into the club without so much as a second glance from the bouncer. The little rumors they started were hilarious:

"I've seen him on TV. Isn't he the Flash?"

"Oh. My. God. That's the *Peaky Blinders* guy. He's so hot!"

My personal favorite was, "Holy shit. That's the guy from *Lubed Up*, that new porn where the guy has a twelve-inch . . ."

Is it normal to relish being confused for a horse-hung porn star? Probably not, but I didn't care. I loved every minute of it. The rumors of my equine parts only made them want me more once I got inside.

The walk of fame was the sizzle before the steak was served. I loved meat.

"Hey, Ty." The twenty-something guy behind the counter collecting covers waved up at me. I flashed him a smile, then leaned across and gave him a peck on his cheek. It turned brilliant red the moment I pulled back, and his eyes widened.

"Good to see you too, Perry."

I pressed forward without giving him time to recover. Flashes of light and lasers flowed down the darkened walkway, drawing me toward the dance floor like a moth to a flame. The walls vibrated as music blared, rattling framed photos of years of patrons. I paused as I passed several containing my image: dancing shirtless on a box, dancing shirt-less with a local TV newscaster, dancing shirtless between a couple, one of whom played in the NFL.

That was one of my all-time best nights. Mason, the football player, had been traded to a team out west. San Francisco, I think. I hadn't seen or heard from them since that night. They put the "hot" in "hot as fuck," and that night, I supplied the "fuck."

I sighed at the memory.

"Hey, handsome. You going in, or should I skip all this and take you home right now?"

I turned to find a blond, muscular dude who'd already taken his shirt off. My eyes roamed his body, and my lips curled in appreciation. He was confident to the point of cocky. I liked that, but I didn't want him to know it.

Let the games begin.

"Nice. I just got here. Look for me inside."

I turned and strode down the hallway, glancing back once before vanishing onto the dance floor. From his stunned expression, Blondie wasn't used to having to hunt for his meals.

Two hours later, my body was bathed in sweat as I danced atop a box to the pulsating beat of some European techno. Half-naked men crammed in as tightly as possible swayed around me. One of the bartenders had given me a diamond-embossed pink pill an hour earlier, and the world spun as warmth tickled my skin.

I was an island in a churning sea of flesh and muscles.

My cock hardened in my jeans, throbbing to the heartbeat of the club. I ran my hands across my chest, smearing the saltiness, teasing my nipples and skin. Every sensation caused my pulse to race faster. I opened my eyes and the strobing lights beat against me. I reached for them, enchanted, but the firm grip of a palm against my groin snapped my head downward—but I didn't pull away. The pressure, the heat, it all felt amazing. I pressed myself against the man's grasp, willing him to stroke against the tight denim.

"Get down here," a deep voice commanded.

I squinted. He looked familiar. Cropped brown hair, square jaw, ridiculously wide shoulders, and broad, hairy chest. And dimples. I knew those dimples. My favorite NFL player had dimples like those.

I grabbed his hand and pressed it against my cock, while accepting his other hand and lowering myself to the dance floor. His eyes never left mine. They held the same dilated desire that filled my chest with every breath.

"Fuck, I was hoping we'd find you tonight." Another muscular body pressed against me from behind, and two hands reached around to grip and knead my chest. Teeth grazed my neck before lips pressed into my skin. The music changed to a faster, more primal beat. It was more a ritual refrain than a melody. The lights dimmed, leaving only red lasers piercing the darkness.

"Mason, god—"

The footballer grinned. "I'll be your god tonight. Now shut up and kiss me."

His mouth smothered mine. His arms wrapped around me and pulled his husband tight against my back. Behind me, Diego's kisses grew passionate, urgent. His tongue devoured my sweat, and he pulled my skin with his teeth.

My dick throbbed against Mason's, while Diego's dick ground against my ass.

I sucked in air; Mason's air. It filled me.

I wanted *him* to fill me.

My roll kicked in again, and everything flared to new life.

Waves of heat and sensation coursed through my veins. The wiry fur of Mason's chest brushed against my skin, and I swear I could feel every strand. Diego's teeth and lips descended to between my shoulder blades, while Mason lowered his mouth to tease a nipple.

The lights.

The beat.

Diego's teeth and hands.

Mason's iron grip. His chest and abs.

Over and over, the feelings crashed against me like waves battering a breaker.

I wanted to break, to be washed away in this rapturous storm.

"Fuck, Mason," I groaned.

Mason lifted his head and thrust his tongue in my mouth, then shoved something in my pocket.

Diego whispered from behind, "We're at the Lowes near Vanderbilt. Room 802. Don't make me ask."

"Let's go now. Please," I begged.

Shit, I *never* begged.

Mason growled, then leaned across my shoulder and said something to Diego. The fucker gripped my cock so hard I couldn't focus enough to hear what he'd said.

Without a word, Mason turned and led me by the hand off the dance floor. Diego didn't release my shoulders until he opened the door of a convertible Ferrari and shoved me into the back seat.

Chapter 5

TYLER

Sam flipped a burger, and a sizzle was followed by the mouthwatering aroma of grilled meat. Dom sat dutifully by the side of the grill, his eyes never wavering as the chef worked.

"Dom would make a great cop," Miguel said before taking another pull on his beer. We sat at a picnic table a few paces from where Sam worked his magic.

"Until the criminals have treats. That little shit takes bribes from anyone."

Miguel grunted. His eyes rarely left Sam's backside.

"You're pretty fixated on a treat yourself, mister."

Miguel's grin widened. As if on cue, Sam glanced over his shoulder and winked.

"I don't know if I'm more in awe or disgusted by you two. I might feel the onset of diabetes from all the sweetness floating around," I quipped.

Sam shook his head and turned back to the grill. Miguel gripped my forearm.

"He's the best thing that's ever happened to me. And look at that ass."

"Oh god, please. I'd rather not. It's *Sam*."

"Uh-huh," he growled, as if he could see through Sam's jeans.

A moment passed before Sam scooped the burgers onto a plate and joined us at the table. Miguel already had a giant bowl of tater tots and bucket full of iced beer bottles arranged in the center.

"Time to eat. Who's hungry?"

Dom barked, and the three of us laughed.

I watched as Sam laid a patty on the bun Miguel had spread across his plate, then leaned down and gave him a kiss on his cheek. Miguel leaned in, reveling in the affection. The pair met a couple years ago when somebody screwed up and sent a car from a crime scene to Sam's garage instead of their usual mechanic. Miguel had Sam flummoxed from the moment their eyes met, and I'd watched my best friend fall madly in love in the months that followed. Nearly past the honeymoon phase, their unfettered adoration continued to deepen and grow, with no end in sight.

When they first got together, I was a little worried I'd just lost my best friend, but Miguel surprised me. As inseparable—and insufferable—as those two were, he'd insisted I was family long before he came along and that shouldn't change. My friendship with Sam deepened with the addition of Miguel, somehow strengthening and evolving into a brotherhood I'd never experienced, not even with my own family. I'd never admit it to them, but I loved and admired them both, almost as much as I loved Dom.

"You're thinking. I'm not used to that." Sam bumped me with his hip as he leaned over to serve a burger onto my plate.

"Sorry, not thinking, just tired."

"Ah, okay. That makes a lot more sense. That's my Ty."

"Fuck you," I said through a laugh. Miguel grinned as he munched, then his expression sobered. "You feel alright?"

I cocked my head. "Yeah, fine. Just had a long night."

"Your pupils are dilated."

Sam, sat across from me, watched as Miguel shifted fully into cop mode.

I shrugged. "It's bright out here."

Miguel gave me that dad look, the one that clearly communicates, *Son, I know you're lying.*

I held up my palms. "I had a fun night. What can I say?"

Sam shot Miguel a glance.

"Ecstasy, if I had to guess," Miguel answered his unspoken question.

I cleared my throat. "Uh, guys, I'm right here."

They looked back to me, but said nothing. My parents were pissed.

"Come on. It's not—"

"It *is* a big deal, if that's what you were about to say." Miguel set his burger down. "I see it all the time. Kids buy that shit, having no idea where it was made or what's in it, from dealers they don't know. That's a lot of unknowns to put in your body. More times than not, those pills are cut with other drugs to enhance the effect or reduce the amount of the core drug the dealer has to use in each pill. Who knows what you swallowed last night?"

"Oh, I swallowed a lot more than pills last night."

Sam spat his beer. Miguel was a statue.

"Miguel—"

"Ty, we love you. You're family. Just be careful, okay?"

Of all the things he could've said, the things I expected him to say, that stunned me into silence. I knew we were family, and I knew we cared about each other, but to say it out loud ... I grabbed my beer and tried to clear the lump forming in my throat. Eye contact was suddenly an Olympic sport.

"You could try dating for a change." Sam waded into the water.

I hated this conversation. We'd had it a million times. "Sam, shit, I'm having fun now, not thinking about getting stuck with one person."

They glared.

"Crap, sorry. I didn't mean . . . you guys are perfect. Really." They let me squirm a few seconds. "I'm really happy right now. Can I just enjoy being young and hot for a while?"

"Don't you turn thirty in a few months?" Sam raised a brow.

"So?"

"In gay years, that's getting up there. Should we get you a walker?"

I rolled my eyes. "Let me take my shirt off and have you say that again. I've got a long time before age is a problem. Trust me."

Miguel leaned in. "You'll always get attention, Ty. Hell, you'll probably get laid more than any mattress store in town. But . . ."

I smirked. "Sounds like a lot of fun to me."

"Doesn't it ever feel shallow?" Miguel asked.

"Shallow? I'm just having a good time while I'm young and fit. The club makes me feel alive, and sex is like a Fourth of July fireworks show, especially on X."

Miguel sat back, but didn't say any more.

Sam leaned forward. "Ty, I know you. You put on this big front, but—"

"What front? Come on, Sam, I loved the circuit before we ever met. It's not like I just stumbled into a bar last week."

"Don't you ever get lonely? I can't remember you ever mentioning the same guy twice. Or couple. Or—"

I laughed. "The couple I banged last night was a repeat, thank you very much."

Sam rolled his eyes. Miguel gaped. He was a bit of an altar boy when it came to sex and relationships.

"When's the last time you went on a date?" Miguel asked.

"You mean the whole dinner-and-a-movie thing?"

"Whatever. Could be. Sure."

I had to think a moment. They exchanged a glance while I dug through my memory bank.

"Was it before we met?" Sam asked.

I started to answer, then closed my mouth. Shit. He was right—and we'd met eight years ago. They watched me squirm in my seat. Miguel eventually grabbed his burger and took a bite. Sam sat quietly, his gaze as unwavering as Dom's when I have a pocket full of treats.

"I guess, yeah, maybe a year before." I'm not sure why my voice dropped and chin drooped, but I suddenly felt . . . something . . . and I didn't like it.

"Enough of that. When the right guy comes along, you'll be helpless, and we'll be there to watch you fall flat on your pretty face." Sam finally set his beer down and grabbed a tot. "If you think we give you shit now, just wait till that happens. You'll beg for mercy."

"Like Mason did last night?" I gave him my best lecherous grin.

"God, you're impossible. Eat your damn lunch so words stop coming out of your mouth."

"Yes, Mom." He threw the tater tot he'd intended to eat right at my forehead. Dom snatched it before it could hit the ground.

It was a relief when the conversation turned to the NFL and the Titans' upcoming season. That made me think about my football player, and something other than Dom stirred below the table.

Damn, they'd been a fun couple. It was too bad they lived across the continent or I might want—

Fuck. The rest of that thought made me shiver. What *would* I want? To see them again? For a third time? I chided myself for such a stupid thought. Hooking up with them wasn't the same as seeing a guy over and over. These guys were hookups, just hot sex, nothing more. They didn't mean anything, no matter how many times we met.

Then, without thinking, the image of that guy from the coffee shop flashed into my head. Gabe? Yeah, that was his name. Dom loved him, more than any stranger I could remember in a long time. I could see his head nuzzled snugly in Gabe's lap as he slept. A strange sensation tickled the skin of my chest at that image. I wasn't sure what it was, but it felt like somebody had wrapped a warm blanket around my shoulders.

What the hell?

Chapter 6

TYLER

Mornings sucked, but Monday mornings took sucking to a whole different level.

When I hit snooze for the third time, Dom decided to take matters into his own paws and began stabbing me with his paw.

"Dom, stop. Daddy needs a little more sleep."

Jab. Jab, jab.

I rolled from my side onto my back to put more distance between us.

He took that as an invitation and leapt directly onto my chest and began hopping.

"Oh god, Dom. That hurts," I whined, and curled into a fetal ball. Dom proceeded to rim my ear. Lesbians across the globe would've been jealous of Dom's skills.

I was revolted . . . but I was awake.

Furry fucker.

"Fine. You win," I groused as I poured my lifeless body out of bed. Dom pranced and darted in merry circles around me like a kid at a maypole. How could any creature be so perpetually happy? And on a Monday morning at that?

I fed him first, then showered. Sunday had been a lazy day of baseball on television, and the offensively large pile of laundry in my closet remained dirty—and offensively large. I grabbed the last shirt I'd worn, a gray T-shirt with my all-time favorite band, Journey, scrawled in late twentieth-century script across the chest, and gave it the time-proven man test: I sniffed it.

It didn't kill me, so I assumed I was stronger for the effort and threw it over my head.

Fully clothed and still half-awake, I took Dom outside to do his morning business, then made a sandwich for lunch and headed to my truck. Thankfully, my trusty Ford knew the way to Buddy Brew on its own, so no thinking was required on my part.

"Morning," an equally sleepy-sounding kid behind the counter said when it was my turn. "Whatcha havin' this morning?"

"I need a double of something kick-ass. Just wake me up, okay?"

He chuckled and nodded, then vanished behind the towering grinder to make my brew. I moved to the pickup counter and glanced around while I waited. There was a steady line for takeaway, both in the drive-through and inside the store, but only a couple of tables were occupied. Four employees struggled to keep up with the flow.

The kid slid a bucket-sized cup, with a barely legible *Ty* scrawled in black Sharpie, across the counter. "Double espresso plus mocha and skim milk, add whip and chocolate shavings."

"Shit. You know me."

He grinned. "Just doin' my job, ma'am."

My two conscious brain cells refused to collide, and he vanished before I could make a sharp retort. I took a sip and nearly fell backward at the jet fuel he'd made. The chocolate almost covered the vile taste of liquid lightning . . . almost.

I'd made it halfway to the door when a familiar voice called above the grinders and music. "Ty, wait up."

I turned to see Woody slipping through the half-door that separated the baristas from their customers. His eyes were nearly as bright as his smile. If I didn't like the guy so much, I would've hated him in that moment for being so damn chipper.

"Hey, dude. You sure are popular," he said as he gave me a fist bump, then half-hug.

"Huh? Seriously not, but thanks."

"Well, somebody came looking for you twice yesterday; once in the morning, then again in the afternoon. Left you a note."

He handed me a folded piece of paper that had been sealed with Scotch tape. "Dom" was written in cursive in blue ink, and a tiny paw print was drawn off to the side.

I was too foggy to connect the dots, so Woody leapt to the rescue. "Gabe sure was serious about finding you. I've never seen that guy so much as flirt with anyone outside the deaf group."

A grin stretched my cheeks. I got my share of attention when I went out, but I couldn't remember the last time someone had gone to such effort to track me down. A tiny voice in my head thought it was a tad creepy, but I bitch-slapped that ho back into silence and tore open the note.

Dom,

I heard your daddy took you to the park this weekend. Mine went there without me. I was sad.

My daddy hasn't stopped talking about you and Tyler since. He said your daddy is really handsome and has a great smile.

Did they behave? You know how humans get when they're excited. I hope they didn't try to hump or anything. My daddy gets so embarrassed when I do that to other dogs.

Anyway, I'd really like to meet you next time our daddies have a park day. Maybe they'll take us to a dog park so we can play.

I love to run. Do you like to run?

Tell your daddy to call mine sometime, okay?

Audie

An actual pawprint was pressed into the page beneath the name.

I lost track at how long I stared at the note. He hadn't told me he had a dog. Audie? A deaf guy's dog was named *Audie*? I couldn't suppress a laugh. People in the back of the coffee line turned.

Then Gabe's face popped into my head, and I could see his dimples deepen as he watched me stare at his handiwork. I was already a little blown away that he came looking for me. Writing a note from his dog to mine pushed everything to a differ-ent level of clever and cute. I didn't even know the guy and it felt like my heart was doing the same racing-in-circles thing Dom had done earlier.

"Dude, if you grin any wider, your face is gonna split."

"Sorry." I folded the note and shoved it in my jeans pocket. I wanted to giggle or laugh or pump my fist . . . something.

"What? Gonna leave me hangin'?"

"I . . . it's . . . well . . . he just said hi."

Woody rolled his eyes. "Alright. Whatever. Do you need to pass a note back while the teacher's out of the classroom?"

"Nope. I have his number now." I patted my pocket, winked, and practically skipped out of the shop.

Chapter 7

GABE

M ondays were funny.

People took their dogs to the park over the weekend and realized how poorly behaved they were. That meant a rush in the first few hours of every week as they committed to sending them to school as quickly as possible. They failed to understand one basic but very important idea: most of the time, it was the human who needed training, not the dog. But try telling that to a professional used to having others follow their orders.

This Monday was no different.

"Tam, you mind taking check-ins? I need to go monitor the pack."

Tamara and I met on my third day in America. I was nineteen years old, deaf, gay, and new to the country and culture. I'd always been a great lipreader, but only had a rudimentary understanding of English, and most hearing people didn't realize that sign language wasn't the same around the world. Sure, some signs were similar, but many were completely different, just like spoken or written language. It was bad enough to struggle to understand hearing people when they spoke, but to have a language barrier separating me from other deaf people was almost unbearable.

I've never felt so lost and alone as I did in those first few years in the US.

Tam was my one friend who'd stuck with me through everything. She'd spent a freshman semester of college in Rome, and had a passable understanding of Italian. That helped a lot. When we struggled to communicate, she downloaded an app that translated and displayed text. Despite how frustrating those first years were, her friendship never faltered.

Now, she was family.

I don't know if I could've stuck it out without her.

Working together was the most natural thing in the world, and having a hearing person by my side made everything easier, especially for our owners.

The dogs didn't seem to care.

"Got it. Go do your thing, Beastmaster." She rolled her index fingers over each other in the sign for *go* and blew me an overly dramatic kiss.

She'd given me that nickname the first week after we opened Pawsome Academy and Doggy Day Care, and I hadn't been able to shake it since. She even had shirts made with it scrawled above the left breast. Most of our owners didn't know my real name.

Seventeen small-breed dogs played and roamed in one grassy field, while eight larger pups did the same in another. Devin, our other employee, was playing referee from his perch above the center fence that divided the two areas. He waved as I entered the big dog area.

"All good?" I signed.

He gave me a thumbs-up, then signed, "Roxie's worked up today. You might need to pull her out."

"She's got agility training with me at nine. I'll burn off that energy then."

He gave me another thumbs-up, then stepped down to break up a pair of poms who were getting into it over a tennis ball.

The deaf community had interesting fault lines, especially in the United States. Some ardently opposed lipreading, preaching the values of sign language. The other side wanted us to be "more mainstream," which was hearing-impaired code for "normal." They hated sign language because it called attention to our differences, to our particular physical challenge. I honestly didn't understand either side. Lipreading and sign language were tools. Both were useful in the right situation. If I'd had to lipread without using signs, I never could've communicated with Devin from across the yard.

And there were times when I wanted to say something no one else would understand, especially the hearing people around us. Sign language allowed me to do that. Hearing people rarely knew any signs, and even fewer were adept at listening. I didn't really care what other people thought—at least, that's what I told myself.

Three one-hour training sessions later, I sat at the front counter with Tamara.

My phone buzzed and flashed.

UNKNOWN NUMBER: HEY. IT'S TYLER. CAN YOU GIVE AUDIE A MESSAGE FROM DOM? HE'S DOING BUTTON TRAINING, BUT MY PHONE'S KEYBOARD IS STILL TOO SMALL FOR HIS PAWS.

I barked out a laugh. I hadn't expected a text from Tyler, and certainly hadn't thought he'd carry my dog-note-gag further.

Tam tapped my arm for me to look up. "Oh, this must be good. Spill."

"Hang on. Let me reply."

I saved the number, creating a nickname I could remember, thought a moment, then typed.

> ME: SURE. AUDIE'S BEEN GETTING IM-PATIENT. YOU SHOULD TEACH DOM IT'S RUDE TO KEEP A LADY WAITING.

> DOM'S DAD: WE'LL WORK ON THAT. LOL DOM WANTS AUDIE TO KNOW HE'D LOVE A PLAY DAY AT THE DOG PARK, AND HUMANS ARE INVITED, BUT THEY SHOULD LEAVE THE ICE CREAM AT HOME. TWEETY GETS THE DOGS ALL WORKED UP.

> ME: GOT IT. ICE CREAM IS FOR HUMAN TIME.

Tam tapped my arm again. "What? Your cheeks are about to pop." She made an explosion like her fingers were blowing out of her cheeks.

I grinned and nodded. "His name's Tyler. I met him at the coffee shop. Well, we didn't actually meet. I saw him there, then we ran into each other at Centennial on Saturday. He was there with his dog."

Her eyes widened. "A man *and* a dog? You've been holding out on me."

I chuckled. "Hardly. I didn't even get his number, had to leave a note at the coffee shop and hope he would call."

"You left him a note? Aww, Peaches, that's so sweet."

I hated when she called me Peaches. That made her do it more.

"When are you seeing him again? When can I meet him?" I could feel the excitement vibrating in her voice.

"Calm your cannoli. This is our first conversation. Can we have one date before you waterboard the poor guy?"

"Cannoli? You going full Italian on me now?" She grinned, then held up her index finger. "One date, then he's mine."

I shook my head, then did the only acceptable thing: I gave in.

"Yes, ma'am."

"Well, don't keep the man waiting." She motioned to my phone like I'd been the one distracting her. When I glanced back down, there were three more messages.

DOM'S DAD: SO, DOG PARK FIRST DATE?

DOM'S DAD: WE'RE THERE PRETTY MUCH EVERY NIGHT AFTER WORK. DOM'S REALLY ANXIOUS TO MEET AUDIE.

DOM'S DAD: I THINK HE HAS A CRUSH.

ME: LOL THEY HAVEN'T EVEN MET. HOW CAN HE HAVE A CRUSH?

DOM'S DAD: I DON'T KNOW. I WAS KINDA CRUSHING IN THE COFFEE SHOP BEFORE WE MET.

ME: NO WAY. REALLY?

DOM'S DAD: DON'T GET SIDETRACKED HERE. YOU FREE AFTER WORK?

ME: TONIGHT?

DOM'S DAD: DOM WON'T REST UNLESS WE GO. I'LL BE THERE NO MATTER WHAT, BUT WOULD RATHER BE THERE WITH YOU.

DOM'S DAD: SHIT. WAS THAT CHEESY? I SUCK AT THIS. I DIDN'T MEAN ... NEVER MIND. TONIGHT?

ME: I THINK YOU'RE CUTE. YES, TONIGHT.

Shit. Had I just sounded too eager? He must think I'm such a goober. I'm so bad at this.

DOM'S DAD: SURE. CAN'T WAIT. DOM WILL PROBABLY WET HIMSELF WHEN HE SEES YOU AGAIN.

ME: I MIGHT PIDDLE MYSELF IF YOU WEAR THAT TIGHT SHIRT AGAIN.

DOM'S DAD: MAYBE I'LL JUST TAKE IT OFF.

ME: DON'T YOU DARE MAKE ME PEE ALL OVER THE DOG PARK. I'LL NEVER FORGIVE YOU.

DOM'S DAD: HA. FAIR ENOUGH. NO PIDDLING ON A FIRST DATE.

DOM'S DAD: SIX O'CLOCK? TWO RIVERS PARK?

ME: PERFECT. OH, GUESS I SHOULD WARN YOU: AUDIE'S A GERMAN SHEPHERD, AND SHE'S A BIG GIRL, SCARES A LOT OF PEOPLE.

DOM'S DAD: DOM ISN'T SCARED OF ANYTHING. WE'LL BE FINE. BESIDES, I'M PRETTY GOOD WITH DOGS.

ME: YEAH, I'M OKAY WITH THEM TOO.

I hadn't told him what I did for work yet, which made that little exchange even funnier.

DOM'S DAD: HEY, GOTTA GET BACK TO WORK. SHOP'S BUSY TODAY. WHAT IS IT WITH MONDAYS?

ME: I FEEL YA. SEE YOU AT SIX.

I couldn't wipe the goofy grin off my face as I set my phone on the counter. It took a moment to realize Tam was still sitting nearby—and staring a hole through me.

"What?" I feigned innocence.

"Listen, you little shit, you're keeping man meat from me. That's against the code."

"Code?" I laughed. "When did we adopt a code?"

"The minute you met me. It's implied. And no, you'll never get a copy, that way I can change it as often as I like."

I sat in the wheely chair opposite her. "What good's a code if you can just snap your fingers and change it? Shouldn't rules be static?"

"Nope. Absolutely not. Now, enough of that. Spill. What is this man planning to do with my Poo Bear?"

"God, not Poo Bear again. Can we go back to Peaches? Or Beastmaster? At least that makes me sound manly."

She snorted. "You're half my weight soaking wet. Making you look manly is a lost cause."

"Thanks a lot." I puffed out my chest, which only made her laugh harder. "Fine. We're meeting at the dog park tonight so Audie and Domino can meet."

"Domino?"

"Yeah. Black-and-white border collie. Super smart and cute. You'd like him. Ty calls him Dom."

"And you just called him Ty."

I shrugged. "It's what most people call him—at least, that's what Woody told me."

"Woody the barista? Please tell me you're not taking man advice from Music City's own surfing slut?"

"Hey! Woody's a—"

"Slut. I'm surprised he doesn't leave a lube trail like a slug or some crustacean."

"You're really gross, you know that?" I moaned through another laugh. "Besides, crustaceans don't leave trails."

"If you say so. You're the guy taking dating advice from one."

She hopped out of her chair and darted out the back door before I had a chance to reply. Something juvenile in my brain forced my eyes down to see if she had, indeed, left a trail.

There would be a special place in therapy for me one day.

Chapter 8

TYLER

"**W**hy are you pacing around that car? You're making me nervous with all your prancing."

I grinned up as Sam glared at me from his office doorway. He'd been my boss and best friend for years, but it still amazed me how he could read my mood from across the shop.

"Sorry, just thinking."

One of his brows raised. "That's definitely not like you. Hookup go bad or something? Get some poor guy pregnant?"

"We'd go on TV if that happened. Hell, I wouldn't have to work for you anymore, might even buy this place from you."

"You don't do anything other than screw, work, play with Dom, and go to the gym. It *can't* be your boss. He's amazing."

"My boss is kind of a prick, but he's alright." I rolled my eyes and tossed the wrench I'd been clutching into a toolbox. "Dom is awesome, best dog ever. And I never said this wasn't about a guy, just not about one I've hooked up with."

Sam's other brow rose, and he left the comfort of his doorway to lean against the car I was supposed to be working on.

"Who has you all twisted up? You haven't had a second date in all the years I've known you, much less met a guy who made you pine."

"I'm not pining."

"Like a lost puppy missing his mom. I wouldn't be surprised if you started whimpering."

I shoved his shoulder playfully. The fucker didn't budge, but I stumbled backward.

"More time in the gym will fix that too," he teased.

"That's workplace harassment. Hostile work environment? Something like that."

"What can I say? I like it rough." He grinned, shrugged, then glanced down at his watch. "That job isn't due until tomorrow afternoon. Let's knock off and grab a beer. You can tell me all your dirty little secrets."

"Wish I could, but, well, I kind of have a date tonight."

Sam's brows had relaxed but now shot to the ceiling.

"This is a second date, isn't it? Holy shit. Is Nashville's playboy getting soft?"

"Can't be a playboy if you're soft, Sam."

He crossed his arms and gave me the same look my dad gave when he'd caught me with a cigarette in my mouth but I still denied smoking.

"Fine. His name's Gabe. We're meeting at the dog park. Technically, this is our first date, so my record remains unblemished."

"Dog park? Shit, you're not just hooking up, are you?" He stared a beat. "What do you mean *technically* a first date?"

"We saw each other at Buddy Brew, then sort of ran into each other at Centennial. This is the first time we've planned to meet up."

"Huh. Okay. The judges agree: this is a first date. The Russian judge objected, but no one listens to her anymore."

"You're such an asshole," I said through a chuckle.

"And you love me for it." He turned to head back into his office. "I'm closing up. I'll want details tomorrow."

"Yes, Mom."

His head whipped around, and he growled, "I'm all daddy, and you know it."

Images of Sam slamming his cop–boyfriend Miguel against the shop's metal wall flashed before me. If Sam hadn't been like a brother . . .

I smacked my cheek to clear my mind of things it *definitely* shouldn't be seeing, then packed up my tools. There was a dog park waiting.

Dom started whimpering the moment I turned into the park's lot. His head bobbed back and forth as he bounced from one playing dog to the next. There were a dozen pups in the large breed area, most clumped around the owners standing under a large shelter. One owner and his dog in the far corner caught my eye. The massive German shepherd sat patiently before its human, then leapt to obey whatever command he'd issued before returning to sit before him again with rapt attention. Dom was attentive and generally obedient, but that pair was playing on another level.

Then the owner turned from the dog toward the lot. It was Gabe.

Damn. He said he was good with dogs, but . . . damn.

We entered the double gate and I released Dom to be greeted by a welcoming committee of curious pooches. Tails wagged. Butts were sniffed. In all, it was a warm greeting. Then the pack lost interest in the new arrival and darted in all directions to find other things to sniff or pee on. Dom followed a snowy retriever. A moment later, they gave each other the universal play bow and became a blur of fur streaking across the grass.

Abandoned by my best friend, I made the trek across the ground to where Gabe was. His beast ignored everything and everyone, remaining singularly focused on Gabe. When I was within a few paces, her ears perked up and her eyes darted toward me, but a "tsk" from Gabe snapped her attention back to her human.

Gabe didn't turn from his dog, and I decided to play spectator until he did. It was fun watching someone who was so clearly skilled work their magic.

With one gesture, the dog sat. With another, she stood on her hind legs. With a third, she leapt into the air and did a backflip.

"Holy shit. Did she just do a backflip?" I said, then remembered Gabe couldn't hear me.

He must have sensed my presence. He turned, and a wide grin parted his lips.

"Hey. This is Audie." He ruffled the German's neck. "Audie. Hug. Go."

Before I could blink, a mountain of fur planted its paws on my chest and began licking my chin. I nearly fell backward under her weight. I loved dogs, but couldn't help a spike of fear as her teeth grazed my skin between licks.

Gabe watched with giggling eyes, finally saying, "Audie. *Casa.*"

Audie fell from my chest, closed the gap in two strides, and sat at Gabe's feet, looking up at him for her next command.

I shook my head in wonder. "You guys are amazing. Did you train her?"

Gabe nodded. "We started with simple attention and name drills when she was about two months old."

"Wow. That young?"

He shrugged. "She's smart. Dogs can do a lot more than we give them credit for. We just have to challenge them and be very, very patient."

Dom finally remembered Daddy was at the park and checked in. Fear wasn't a word in his vocabulary, and he strode up to Audie and proceeded to sniff her seated tail. Audie glanced back, then decided Dom wasn't interesting and continued scanning the park.

"Guess they get along okay," I said.

"Audie gets along with pretty much everybody. That's another benefit of training at an early age, especially with a lot of other dogs around."

"You have more dogs?" My eyes widened.

He laughed. "Something like that. I own a dog training academy."

"No shit? You're a professional trainer?"

He nodded.

"That's so cool. But—" I stopped myself before inserting my foot.

He grinned again. "How do I do that being deaf? Is that what you were going to ask?"

Now I felt like shit again. I nodded.

"Dogs learn differently than humans. We want to talk them to death. They learn through smell and sight *before* sound. Hand gestures are a lot more effective than verbal cues. Pretty perfect for a deaf guy, don't you think?"

His smile was so freakin' infectious, and his dimples had little smiles of their own. His ability to wipe away my embarrassment was a magic all its own.

"Okay, back to dogs. I can't believe you're a real dog trainer," I said with childlike glee. "A minute ago you used the word *casa* with Audie. What was that?"

My brows scrunched, and he laughed. "I use Italian words for things I don't want confused by English speakers."

"Really?"

He nodded. "Say Audie and I were out for a walk and someone started following us. If I said the Italian word for *shield,* she'd go into protect mode. Anyone who approached me with a whiff of bad energy would regret it."

He knelt down to face Audie, gave her a kiss on her nose, then said, "*Adare.*"

Audie bolted away from us. Dom followed, and they were soon chasing each other playfully around the park.

"That's my version of a *release* command, letting her go play or do whatever she wants."

"How many words does she know?" I asked.

"Words? Who knows? Like I said, we underestimate them. We probably share fifty or so commands."

"Holy cow. That's incredible."

"Audie's the best."

We watched the dogs play a moment without speaking. There was something peaceful standing in the park, surrounded by carefree animals enjoying their freedom. I sucked in the cool autumn air and blew out a contented sigh. When I glanced back to Gabe, he was staring at me. My eyes fell to my shoes, and my cheeks colored.

Am I twelve? What the hell?

"So, uh, why use Italian?" I asked.

"It's my native language. I moved here from Italy when I was nineteen."

"Really? That must've been something."

"Yeah. That's for sure." He nodded slowly and his eyes drifted, then he motioned toward a nearby bench. He was quiet a moment after we sat, then turned to face me. "My parents and brother were a world away, and I found myself in a foreign country, surrounded by people who spoke a different language I couldn't even hear. I'm sure it's a challenge for hearing people to visit a place where everyone speaks something different, but try lipreading a foreign tongue."

Something in his pained expression made my heart ache. I barely knew what to say.

"But you sign, right? I saw you and that guy at Centennial. That had to help."

He gave me that smile a mother gives a child who, after the fifth explanation, still doesn't get it.

"It's a different language, and many of the signs are different. I'd hoped the deaf community would be forward-thinking enough to have some basic commonality. Sadly, that was too much to hope for.

"My English was rudimentary at best, so writing down conversations or using iPhone translators only helped a little. Besides, who has an English-to-Italian translation app downloaded and ready for when they run into the new deaf guy?"

"Gabe, wow. That must've been terrifying."

His eyes found some distant point beyond the fence as he spoke. "I was eighteen and had never felt so alone, so detached from everyone around me."

"How did you do it?" I asked.

His eyes found mine again, and he cocked his head.

"How did you made that adjustment? God, I can't imagine how hard that must've been."

He gave me a tight smile. "I met Lucas the first week I moved to the United States. He's the guy you saw at Centennial. He found me sitting in the corner of Buddy Brew gripping an untouched cup of espresso and fighting back tears that threatened to drown anyone who came near. I don't know how he knew I was deaf before we spoke, but he did. He tried to sign, but I couldn't understand a word. Then he whipped out a pad and began writing. The confusion on my face sparked pity in his. Finally, an idea struck and he darted back to his table, scooped up his laptop, and opened Google Translate as quickly as his fingers could type. We entered short, five or six-word phrases, and were rewarded with a really rough imitation of conversation—but it *was* a conversation.

"I'd never been so happy to hear a computerized voice absolutely murder my mother tongue."

I thought it was odd he'd said he'd *heard* the computer, but ignored it and said, "He sounds like a good guy."

"I don't know what I would've done if Lucas hadn't craved a mocha cappuccino that night. In a matter of moments, he became my second brother, my American brother, and the best friend I could've hoped for."

"Did you two ever—?" I couldn't help myself.

"Luc? Really? Lord, no!" He barked a throaty laugh, and I found myself chuckling with him. "He's a great guy, but he's the oldest thirty-nine-year-old on the planet. There aren't many guys out there who could put up with his crusty ass."

"Eww. You said crusty ass. That's gross." My inner third grader popped out.

It took a second, then Gabe giggled. Deep creases formed around his eyes as he laughed, and I swear, the brown in his irises brightened.

Dom saved me from saying anything stupid, racing up to our bench and bouncing into my lap. By the time Audie arrived, I was slathered in slobber. Audie shamed my ill-mannered beast by sitting before Gabe and patiently awaiting his affection, casting an occasional glance at us as if wondering why we were so poorly behaved.

Great. Now a dog thinks I'm too wild. Sam would love this.

I wasn't sure where that thought came from. I hadn't given the boys' lecture much thought since leaving their place. That conversation suddenly became a song stuck in my head, replaying its annoying lyrics over and over without mercy. Frustrated with my now spinning brain, I pushed Dom down and signaled for him to sit.

Gabe was watching me again when I looked up. I raised a brow.

"I lost you for a minute. Where did you go?"

Is he really psychic? Crap.

"Uh, nowhere, really. I guess you talking about Lucas made me think about friends."

He motioned to Audie and she placed both paws on his lap so he could rub her head. "Tell me about your friends."

"Well, okay. Sam owns the garage where I work. We've been best friends for years. Miguel's his boyfriend."

Gabe was still stroking Audie's fur and hadn't looked up. When he did, I felt stupid. He hadn't heard me. I repeated what I'd said, and he nodded attentively.

I spent the next few minutes telling him about the guys and how they'd met. He peppered me with questions about the murder case Miguel was working on at the time, fascinated with the real-life crime drama we'd lived through. All that felt like a lifetime ago.

"Okay, so, you're a mechanic. What else? What do you like to do when you're not working?"

God, I hated the dating dance. The questions were always the same, and nobody really cared what the answers were. All they wanted was to get to the good part where both of us were naked and sweaty. Guys at the gym or club—hell, at the grocery store—took one look at me and wanted to screw, and that was great with me. I loved it: the attention and the sex. The fact they rarely wanted anything more was a bonus. Sam and Miguel might've hit the dating jackpot, but, like the ticket says, "The odds of winning are one in a billion." I preferred the sure odds of a happy ending.

I looked into Gabe's eyes as my inner monologue played and found none of that. His eyes didn't roam my body or fixate on my chest or arms. They locked onto mine with an intensity that made me a little uncomfortable. When he read my lips, he leaned forward. Was he doing that to see my words better or . . . was he actually interested in knowing the answers? Guys didn't usually care for details beyond my chest and arm measurements. Was he interested in more than . . . in *me?*

"Well, uh, I go to the gym, and, uh, do stuff with Dom," I said, suddenly self-conscious.

Gabe grinned. "That's obvious. Both are, actually. What else?""Well, I like to go out, I guess."

His brow furrowed.

Shit, did I just say that? What if he doesn't like the bars? He seemed like such a grounded guy. *Did I just—* Then I froze. Was I worried about my clubbing putting this guy off?

What the hell's wrong with me? Why should I care? We just met, and I like to have fun. If he doesn't like that, screw him.

My internal indignance felt *off* somehow. I didn't understand it, and I didn't like how it clawed at my chest.

"Really? I've only been out a few times. I like all the lights and vibrations from the music, but it's hard for me to have a conversation in the dark."

"Oh, right," I said. "Wait, the vibrations of the music?"

He nodded. "Obviously, I can't hear the music, but I can feel the vibrations and how they change with the beat or tone. It helps that they play it so loud. That part's fun."

"Huh," I said artfully.

"My friends don't really like to go out, so we usually just get together at each other's place and cook or play games."

Dom sensed the awkward silence that fell between us and cocked his head.

"When did you learn to lipread?"

Where the hell did that come from? I felt like a complete asshole asking about his hearing. What an idiot.

But Gabe didn't flinch. "I was diagnosed with Usher syndrome when I was a baby, but I didn't start losing my hearing until I was around seven. We knew it was going to happen, just not when or how quickly. My mom and dad got a bunch of books and started teaching me signs before I could talk—at least, that's how they tell it. I guess I was four or five when I went to classes for the first time."

He responded like it was the most ordinary question anyone could ask.

"Did you learn English then too?"

He nodded. "My mom is from Canada originally. She insisted I learn English alongside Italian. I just wish she'd known ASL isn't the same as LIS."

"ASL?"

"Sorry. I forget everybody doesn't know. American Sign Language. LIS is the Italian version, *Lingua dei Segni Italiana*." His sounds altered when he spoke the Italian words, but didn't quite imitate the Italian accent I recognized.

"You had to learn all that? Just to communicate?"

He nodded. "I was little and liked to learn. It was like a game to me back then. People born deaf or who lose their hearing as adults have it a lot worse than I did."

"What do you mean?"

"If you're born deaf, you never know what things sound like. I still remember what words sound like, so it's easier for me. Some words still take practice, and I get funny looks or have to repeat things. But people who lose their hearing all at once never get the chance to prepare like I did. I had years of lessons and coaching before my sound was turned off."

The way he phrased that made me chuckle. "What?"

"I'm so sorry, Gabe. I didn't mean . . . I wasn't laughing at you."

"Did you just picture an Oompa Loompa waddling up to me and flipping off a switch on the back of my head?"

My eyes widened, and now he began laughing.

The dogs growled and barked as they played. Owners chatted, and children on the nearby playground squealed and laughed. A jet rumbled overhead. I wouldn't have normally noticed any of those things, but they thundered in my ears in that moment. I tried to imagine what it would be like, hearing the world around you, knowing one day it would all be turned off. He'd experienced that as a child. He'd lived through that loss and grown into a guy confident enough to move halfway around the world on his own.

And somehow, through it all, he'd managed to keep his sense of humor, to laugh at things that made me cringe, to smile in the face of incredible change and loss. From the short time I'd known him, that smile never wavered, never failed to reach his eyes. There was a joy in him I hadn't seen in many, most of whom would never experience anything that compared to the challenges he encountered every day.

I was suddenly overcome by the strength of this beautiful man standing before me.

I glanced away.

His hand found my arm. "Tyler, it's alright to laugh. You don't have to worry about upsetting me, okay?"

I turned back to find understanding in his eyes. I swallowed a lump and fumbled a question, "So, uh, what about you? When you're not training dogs?"

He quirked a brow, then his smile returned. That awkward change of subject was likely another whiplash he'd grown accustomed to over the years.

"I hang out with our group a lot. Most of the time, we don't do anything special, just eat or play board games. A few times a month we go help with the kids at the deaf school."

"Huh. I didn't even know there was a deaf school in Nashville."

"Yeah, a pretty good one too. The kids are fun."

Gabe really was something. The more I learned, the more I wanted to know. "What else? Sports? Anything athletic? You look like you're in good shape."

He blushed and his eyes darted away before returning to mine. "I play a lot of tennis, and Audie and I run most mornings before work. She's a terror if she doesn't get her exercise."

"Tennis? Sounds fun."

"Do you play?" he asked.

"I own a racquet and can usually keep the ball inside the fence, but that's about it. Are you good?"

"I can hold my own," he said casually. "What about you?"

"Basketball was always my sport. I played in high school and was supposed to play in college . . ."

He waited for me to explain. When I hesitated, he said, "It's okay if you don't want to talk about it."

"Thanks. That's probably a better conversation over a beer or glass of wine."

His eyes sparkled. Had I just asked him out again without realizing it? Today had been fun, but I didn't want to lead him on. There's no way I wanted to date anybody.

I jumped back onto safer ground. "You said you run to give her exercise. Doesn't she get plenty when she goes to work with you?"

"Sure, but that's more play than work for her. We'll run four or five miles and she'll still have a full battery. I'm not sure I could ever really tire her out."

I grunted. "Sounds like another dog I know."

Domino raced up and bowled into me, magically sensing I'd referred to him in conversation. One ear was flopped backward, and his tongue lolled out the side, giving him an almost cartoonish look. Gabe howled with laughter as I tried to keep my balance from my rambunctious beast's assault.

Thankfully, a goldendoodle entered the double gate, and Dom bolted away to greet the park's newest arrival, giving us another moment of peace. I watched in amazement as Audie remained firmly in place. Her gaze followed Dom, then turned up-ward to Gabe. With a gesture from her human, Audie raced away to join the pack. I wondered how long she would've sat patiently by Gabe's side if he hadn't given her permission.

"You really are great with her."

His smile beamed. "I love working with dogs. They make sense to me."

"What do you mean?"

"Dogs are social animals. In the wild, if they want to belong to a pack, they have to follow the pack's rules. Once you understand their rules, they're easy to work with. It's living with humans that messes them up." He shook his head. "Most of my job is fixing dumb stuff humans do with their dogs."

Gabe's passion flowed freely when he spoke. I'd seen how much he loved Audie in their interactions, but hearing him talk about working with other dogs, it was clear his heart was big enough for any pup who wandered his way. Mental images of Dom surrounded by a dozen furry friends danced in my head.

"What are you smiling at?"

Gabe was staring intently when my mind released me back to the present.

"Oh, sorry. Just picturing you with dogs at the academy."

He thought a moment, then said, "You should see it for yourself. Bring Domino. I bet he'd love to play with a real pack."

"Really?"

He nodded, and pearly teeth flashed as his smile widened. "I might like to see Dom's daddy again too."

That tickle in my chest I'd felt when we'd first walked into the park and seen Gabe flared up again. Before I realized what I was doing, my hand was rubbing my sternum.

"You okay?" Gabe's eyes were suddenly narrowed as they fell to my hand.

"Oh, yeah, fine. Sorry. Just, um, had an itch."

Heat flooded my face, and I was sure I'd turned ten shades of red.

Thankfully, Dom darted back toward us, giving me an opportunity to divert my attention and squat to receive his slobbery affection. Audie trailed behind and, without any instruction from Gabe, sat dutifully before him with her eyes lasering into his face. He knelt beside me and began rubbing Audie's ear. Our sides pressed against each other and that damn heat flared again.

I'd lost count of how many insanely hot guys I'd been with. Never once had I been nervous or flustered. Hell, with any of those guys, a brush like that would've started my blood pumping and sent clothes flying.

Why was Gabe's incidental touch suddenly turning me into an awkward teenager again?

"Audie just licked her lips several times. If we don't go home and eat, she'll start punching me with her paw."

I laughed and glanced up. "Dom does the paw punch too. That's too funny."

I'd barely finished the sentence when Dom's nails jabbed into my arm, and Gabe began laughing.

"Dom, attack. Help Daddy. Bite the bad man!"

Gabe laughed harder as Dom stared up at me, confused by commands he'd never heard before.

Out the corner of my eye, I saw Gabe give Audie a quick gesture. In a blink, the massive German had knocked me on my back and was staring down at my face. My useless pup danced around us and barked excitedly. I peeked around the fur mountain to find Gabe wiping away tears.

Chapter 9

GABE

Some days, the pack was restless.

Tamara stood on a wooden box at the center of a dozen rowdy dogs as they wrestled and nipped their way about the pen. She'd already broken up three tussles, and was on high alert for perked ears or spiked fur. I tried to keep my focus on the golden retriever sitting before me. She responded to basic commands well, but had the attention span of a gnat. My goal was to get this hyper monster to stick with the stay command until I released her. We'd nearly exhausted my treat bag, and her eyes still darted to the playpen every time I stepped back. As long as I was in arm's reach, she'd stay in place. That was a victory in itself, but if I took a second step back, she'd bolt to the fence line and whimper to join the others.

Distractions were frustrating.

Two of the smaller dogs went at it and Tam had to hop from her perch to referee the fight. The crazed energy gripped a few of the others, and the yard devolved into a bench-clearing dog brawl. I abandoned the golden and raced into the pen to help.

"Lucy's the culprit," Tam said, as she led a snarling Jack Russell out of the pen. "She's been in a mood since she got here."

"Put her in with Bell. I've done all I can with her for now. We both need a break."

I settled the pack as Tam watched the golden I'd been training quirk her head at the angry little furball who'd just entered her space. While Lucy bared her teeth and squinted her eyes, Bell's face was all curiosity and eagerness. It only took a moment for her good nature to win over the restless terror and turn a confrontation into a play date.

"Why couldn't she just do that in the big pen?" Tam asked, shaking her head as she watched Lucy chase Bell in laps around the pen.

Satisfied the pack was calm, I trudged through to the fence to stand beside Tam and watched a moment. "Lucy needs more exercise. I bet the owner doesn't walk her."

Tam nodded and said something, but her head was turned and I couldn't see what she'd said. She turned with a raised brow, then said, "Sorry. I was asking what else we have today. Any other sessions, or just babysitting?"

"I need to do one more round with Bell, then I'm hitting with Bryan." I glanced down at my watch. "Let's give them another ten minutes and I'll start with her again. Think you can get Lucy to behave once she's burned off some of that energy?"

"Lucy will never burn off enough. She's a tornado." She chuckled. "I'll try. May have to put her inside though."

I started to turn away, but she patted my arm. "How'd it go with that guy? We've been here all day and you haven't said a word."

A grin parted my lips. "It was good. The dogs got along."

She crossed her arms. "Gabriel Giancarlo Rossi, this is the first date you've been on in years and I expect a full report. Don't make me kick your pretty little butt right here in front of all these pups."

"Easy, Mom. No ass-kicking in front of the clients." I laughed and held up my palms. "Tyler's really funny, and Domino—that's his dog—is great.

He's a border collie. With some real training, he could be incredible."

Her eyes narrowed. "You know I don't give two shits about his dog. Get to the good stuff. Was he as hot as you thought in the coffee shop?"

My grin widened. "Hotter. So much hotter."

Tam wouldn't relax until I replayed the whole date. She peppered me with questions and badgered me about finding his picture online, but I refused to become Tyler's stalker. The truth was I hadn't thought of searching for him online. It was actually a good idea, but I didn't want to give her that win. I made a mental note to do some research later.

"When are you seeing him again?" At this point, both her hands gripped my forearms, and she practically vibrated with excitement. If I'd been a bystander watching our conversation, I would've thought she had been the one who went on a great date.

"I don't know. We didn't really set anything up. I invited him to bring Domino here for a play day."

"Yes, yes, yes!" She hopped up and down and clapped her hands. "Then I get to meet him. You know I have to approve before—"

"Oh, I know." I couldn't stop another laugh. "Just don't leave any marks when you waterboard him, please. We can't mess up his pretty face."

She slapped my arm playfully, then leaned in, as though the dogs might hear. "He's really *that* hot?"

I nodded. "Just wait. You'll see."

Bryan texted he was running late for tennis, so I sat in my car with the A/C running and began a death-scroll on TikTok. One guy after another ripped off his shirt to *I Want a Big Boy*. The redundancy was mind numbing, but the muscles were tasty.

Muscles. Hmm.

That made me think of Tyler in his far-too-tight shirt at the dog park. His dark chocolate hair had been mostly tied back, but the same few rebellious locks I'd seen before blew across his forehead in the breeze. He looked like an effing supermodel.

My heart started to race as that damn song played in my mind and Tyler crossed his arms, gripped the bottom of his T-shirt, and began slowly pulling it upward. Abs emerged, one hardened slab at a time. A trail of brown hair parted the rippling sea.

A bead of sweat fell from my forehead into my eye, snapping me out of my daydream. I glanced around the lot, thankful Bry hadn't arrived because my nylon shorts would've revealed more than they covered.

I blew out a breath and tried to calm myself.

Without thinking, I grabbed my phone and sent a text.

> **ME:** HEY. AUDIE SAID TO TELL DOM SHE HAD FUN AT THE PARK.

God, I'm an idiot. Why did I send that? Any self-respecting gay knew to wait at least a day to send a text. What was I thinking? What would *he* think? *He'll probably assume the dumb deaf guy is desperate.*

> **DOM'S DAD:** DOM SAYS HE HAD FUN TOO. HE SAID YOU . . . I MEAN, AUDIE . . . HAS A CUTE BUTT.

I couldn't stop staring at the phone. My cheeks began to ache from the smile that nearly tickled my ears. A giggle slipped out and I smacked the steering wheel, accidentally hitting the horn. A tennis player nearest the lot startled, then turned and gave me a scowl.

I giggled again.

> **ME:** OH, REALLY? DOM NOTICED AUDIE'S BUTT?

> **DOM'S DAD:** YEAH, GUESS SO. ISN'T THAT PRETTY NORMAL FOR DOGS THOUGH? YOU KNOW, THE WHOLE GREETING THING?

> **ME:** SURE. FOR DOGS. DEFINITELY.

A long moment passed. I couldn't take the waiting, so I typed:

> **ME:** ARE YOU DOING THE PARK AFTER WORK?

> **DOM'S DAD:** NO. GONNA BE LATE AT THE SHOP TONIGHT. DOM'S GONNA HATE ME.

ME: YOU COULD MAKE IT UP TO HIM WITH A VISIT TO THE ACADEMY.

Another pause, then dots began dancing. I held my breath.

DOM'S DAD: I'M OFF DAY AFTER TOMORROW. WHAT TIME WORKS BEST?

ME: ANY TIME AFTER TEN. MORNINGS ARE CRAZY WITH CHECK-INS AND GETTING ALL THE DOGS SETTLED.

DOM'S DAD: AWESOME. WE'LL BE THERE AROUND ELEVEN.

Oh . . . my . . . god. We're actually doing this.

I reread the text exchange a dozen times, barely able to sit still in my car.

I hadn't been on many dates. Either guys ran the moment they found out I was deaf—which was pretty much immediately—or I never gave them the chance. Sometimes I wondered if it would be easier to just stay alone, to quit putting myself out there to be disappointed.

The screen pulled me into it again, and my scowl reversed itself. Tyler really wanted to see me again.

Bryan's car pulled into the space beside me, and he waved. I hopped out of my car and headed around to greet him as he climbed out of his, wrapping him in a tight hug.

"Whoa, easy," he signed. He'd been deaf since birth and rarely spoke. He eyed me, then pointed his finger at my face and waved it in a circle. "What's with all this?"

I grinned. "All what? I don't know what you're talking about."

His chin dropped and he stared at me out the top of his eyes. "Asshole."

I giggled. "I'm seeing him again."

"Who?" Then recognition dawned, and his eyes widened. "The hottie?"

I nodded. "He's bringing his dog to the academy for a play day."

Bry rolled his eyes. "That's not a date. That's him using you to give his dog exercise. I bet he asks you to help train too."

"If he just wanted to run Domino, he would go back to the dog park. My academy is pretty far from where he lives."

"And how do you know where he lives?"

My face flushed. "He mentioned it, and I might've accidentally googled him."

"Accidentally?" He laughed and waved a hand in the air. "I'm getting my tennis bag. I can't take any more of you right now." He turned his back to me, silencing anything else I might've said.

As we strode up to the courts, I signed, "He's really nice, Bry."

He put a hand on my arm and stopped walking. "Just be careful, okay? I'm glad you're happy, but—"

"But what?"

He sucked in a breath, then blew it out. "Let's just play tennis, okay? I'm glad you're happy."

I wanted to glare a hole through him, but he turned and walked onto the court, leaving me no choice but to follow.

Chapter 10

TYLER

I shook my head and chuckled as I stuffed my phone back into my pocket.

"What's got you in such a good mood?" Sam asked from his office doorway. "Let me guess. There's another circuit party coming up and you've finally picked out the perfect thong?"

He had my dad's mystical ability to show up any time I was doing something even the slightest bit out of bounds. Texting at work wasn't exactly a crime, but we were backed up, and, while he'd never say anything, I knew it would bother him if he thought I was goofing off.

"Ha ha." I turned back to the car I'd been working on before my phone buzzed. "Yes, there is a party this weekend in Miami. Don't call, text, write, or send smoke signals. I plan to be very unavailable until Tuesday. And for your information, I already own the perfect thong, thank you very much. Two of them."

"For the love of all that's good and holy, *never* let me see them, please."

I grabbed a wrench and laughed. "Was there something you needed, or were you just coming out here where the real work gets done to feel useful? You overhead types are all the same."

"Wait. You were texting. You *never* text; at least, you never reply. You're a lousy communicator." When I didn't respond, I felt his presence as he leaned against the car behind me and lowered his voice. "You were talking to a *man*. Was it that deaf guy you told us about? The one you weren't going to date?"

His voice had a shit-eating grin in it.

"Still not dating," I called from under the hood without looking up. "And yes, it was Gabe."

Sam whistled. "Shit. You called him by name. When's the last time you remembered a hookup's name?"

I straightened, closed the hood, and glanced back as I headed to the driver's-side door. "He's not a hookup."

Sam's eyes widened.

Shit. Now he's going to ask more questions.

"So, if he's not a hookup—"

"He's just a friend who happens to be a dog trainer, and Dom likes playing with his dog."

"Does his dog's daddy like playing with Dom's daddy too?"

I cranked the car's engine and revved it far louder than was necessary. Undeterred, Sam leaned into the window.

"Oh . . . my . . . god!" He tried to mask his gruff voice with a terrible valley girl imitation as he spoke. "You saw him at the coffee shop. That was chance and doesn't count. You ran into each other at the park and bought him ice cream. That's adorable. It sort of counts. Then he left you a note—which was super cute, by the way—and you met for a date. That definitely counts. Has there been another date? Don't make me stick Miguel on the case. You know he'll get to the truth."

He was loving this. I wanted to throw something.

"He invited me to bring Dom to his academy. It's *not* a date."

Sam eyed me long enough to make my skin itch, then turned back toward his office. "If you say so. But I still want details."

I sat with the car running for a long moment, then pulled my phone out again. Gabe's text was still on the screen. As hard as I tried, I couldn't stop a smile from parting my lips.

Chapter 11

GABE

"Okay. Devin is watching the playpen. You've got reception. My one training session is scheduled from ten to eleven o'clock, so I should be done before he gets here. Audie had her run. I stocked the mini fridge with bottles of water in case Tyler wants a drink. What have I missed?"

Tam leaned back in our squeaky chair behind the reception desk. Her eyes shifted like she was watching a tennis match as I paced about the room.

When she didn't respond, I stopped and turned to her. She cocked a brow.

"What?"

"You really like this guy, don't you?"

"I guess."

She laughed and leaned forward to plant her elbows on the desk. "You guess? You look like you're about to wet yourself, and he's still several hours from getting here."

Without thinking, I glanced down at my fly, which only made her laugh harder. For once in my life, I was glad I couldn't hear her.

When I looked back up, she said, "Relax. He wouldn't be coming today if he didn't like you too. If nothing else, maybe he'll be a new customer. We can always use more of those."

I rolled my eyes. "I don't want him to be a customer."

"Oh, I know that. You want to play with his dachshund."

"Tam!"

She smirked. "I bet his weenie dog is—"

"Tamara Louise! I swear, sometimes I wonder why I keep you around."

"Because you need me?" She batted her eyelashes innocently.

"Need is *such* a strong word." I stuck out my tongue in the most mature manner possible, then leaned over the desk. "I bet it's huge."

"Should I tell him a personal inspection is part of the admission process? Like the vax report on the dogs, we need to check out the human too?"

I grinned. "That's a fantastic policy. Strip searches for everyone!"

She mirrored my grin, then stood and peered over my shoulder into the parking lot. "Looks like your ten o'clock just pulled in. That'll give you something to keep your mind off Tyler."

I turned to watch a rail-thin woman struggle as a massive husky dragged her toward the door. Jon Snow was a willful, stubborn, immensely strong dog who rarely got the exercise he needed. His owner lived in perpetual frustration as Jon acted out, often in destructive ways. We'd talked a dozen times about the importance of daily exercise, but some humans refused to listen. Sadly, I knew he'd leave my care in reasonable shape, only to return in a few days with a frenzy in his eyes. I felt sorry for the blue-eyed beast.

"Mind checking them in while I take Jon back?"

She nodded, but her eyes remained on the door. When I turned back, Jon Snow burst through the entrance and nearly knocked me to the floor. I said "Hey!" in a commanding tone, and held out a downward palm. Jon's head snapped up, and his butt smacked to the tiles.

His owner gaped. "I'll never understand how you get him to do that."

"Judy, we really need to schedule a session with the three of us."

"I know. You say that every week. It's just so hard to make the time."

"Whatever we do here won't stick if you don't reinforce it at home." I caught myself before launching into a frustrated lecture, the same one I gave nearly every owner a million times. "Did he get a walk this morning?"

Jon's ears perked up at the mention of the *W* word.

Judy's head shook.

I bit back the reprimand begging to be released and nodded once. "Okay, we'll start with some exercise. See you in an hour."

Jon had more pent-up energy than I'd seen before, and it took nearly twenty minutes of long-distance fetch to tire him out enough to focus. By a quarter to eleven, I was covered in sweat and smelled like a kennel, but Jon's eyes were locked on me as he dutifully obeyed commands.

Red lights attached to each corner of the pen strobed, giving me a five-minute warning before the turning of the hour, so Jon and I turned to head back inside. Something caught Jon's attention, and he bolted ahead of me toward the gate. When I glanced up, I froze. My lips tried to curl upward, but my mouth was suddenly dry.

Jon's nose was stuck as far into the fence as he could shove it as he sniffed the new arrival. Domino danced excitedly, his tail a blur. Tyler was leaning against the fence; he had been watching me train Jon for who knows how long. His hair was unbound and hung near his shoulders. The sleeves of his shirt were rolled up, and the top few buttons were undone. I could just make out a patch of hair peeking out.

He smiled and waved.

Movement behind him drew my eye as Tam signed in exaggerated gestures, "Holy shit, he's hot!" then raced back inside before I could respond.

"Hey," I said as I approached the gate. "Glad you made it."

"Dom wouldn't dare miss a date with Audie."

Did he just call this a date? I nearly fell back-ward.

Unsure how to properly greet a guy on a dog date, I stuck out my hand to shake his. He glanced down, then grinned and took my hand. His grip was firm and warm.

"You been here long?" I asked.

"Ten minutes or so. Long enough to see you at work. You're really good at this."

"Thanks." My heart fluttered. "Um, this is Jon Snow."

He glanced down and chuckled. "But he's not all white. That doesn't make sense."

"I just report the news." I shrugged, then glanced over his shoulder to see if Jon's owner was back. "Jon's mom is always late. Want to let them play a little?"

Domino raced in circles around Tyler's legs at the mention of *play*.

"I think Dom would like that," Tyler said with a grin.

As soon as the gate opened, Dom jetted into the pen and began chasing Jon Snow playfully around the fence line. We watched for a moment as they ran, then slowed so Dom could sniff the boundaries of the new world he'd just entered.

I felt a touch on my shoulder and turned.

"I said, I think they like each other."

"Looks like it. We should get Audie out here too. She loves Jon."

A moment later, Tyler and I stood on the outside of the pen, watching three furry lightning bolts streak across the grass. Dom was fascinated by the tubes and platforms I used with agility training. Jon Snow would occasionally wander away to sniff or mark, but Dom and Audie clung together.

"I've never seen Audie pair like that. She acts like they've been part of a pack for years."

"What can I say? My boy's a stud." Tyler winked, and my pulse kicked up a notch. We were standing close enough that our shoulders pressed against each other.

The red lights flashed again, then remained solid, indicating the end of the session. When I turned to look back, Tam was already approaching with Jon Snow's mom in tow.

"Jon did great today," I said. "But we really need to schedule that session with the three of us. He needs to learn to follow the commands from you, or all this will be for nothing."

Judy's eyes flitted between the playing dogs, Tam, and Tyler, landing on Tyler far more than the others. When her occasional glance turned to an uncomfortable stare, Tam stepped in. "I'll check Jon out. Why don't you give Tyler the tour?"

"Thanks, Tam," I said, grabbing Tyler's arm and leading him away. We'd made it a few paces before I realized I was gripping his bicep and dropped my hand.

Damn, his muscles are hard.

The idea of him being hard . . .

Heat flooded my face.

I glanced at Tyler out the corner of my eye to find a playful grin and darting eyes.

"I, um, I'm not sure there's much to tour. You saw the training pen. It's a lot more fun when I'm working with an agility dog. This is the playpen where we do day care. The office is just off the main entrance, and there's a small kitchen and workroom out back where a groomer rents space. I live in the house over there." Tyler followed my gaze as I pointed to a one-bedroom cottage that sat on the other side of the training pens.

"This is really great, Gabe. How long have you had this place?""Twenty-three."

Tyler turned toward me, his brows knitted together. "Twenty-three?"

"Sorry, what did you ask?"

"How long you've had this place."

"Oh, right. A few years. It took me some time after moving here to find a place and get everything set up."

"Did you always want to be a trainer?"

We'd returned to our spot outside the training pen, and our shoulders were once again pressed against each other. Dom and Audie were playing tug-of-war with a rope toy, ignoring their daddies as we chatted.

"Yeah. I grew up surrounded by a pack. Can't remember ever being without them."

"Really? Your family had a lot of dogs?"

I grinned and shook my head. "We had three. The others were dogs my dad was training. He runs an academy like mine, except he also boards. Some of the more challenging dogs stay with him for months at a time. It can take that long to work the aggression out of some. He's incredible with them."

I wilted under his gaze, and my eyes dropped. When I peeked, he was still staring.

"You miss them, don't you?"

I nodded. "We've always been really close, and moving a world away was rough—still is, some days."

"Why'd you do it? Move, I mean?"

I'd remained around my tight circle so long that nobody had asked me that in a while. I tried to answer, but couldn't find words. Tyler's eyes never left mine.

"I . . . well . . . I guess I wanted something . . . I don't know . . . more. Does that make sense?"

He chuckled and nodded. "I couldn't get out of Pensacola fast enough. I mean, it's a nice enough place, and the beaches are great, but it's a small town. My dad was happy there. I don't remember him ever leaving the county for more than a few

days of vacation. I just couldn't live like that. I needed to see what's out there."

"Exactly." I gripped his forearm without thinking. "Genoa is great. It's stunning, really, but it's not
the world. Italy isn't the world. I had to get out of
there. Besides, the deaf community is a lot larger
here, so there are more opportunities. I would've
ended up working with my dad for the next thirty
years if I'd stayed."

"So instead, you came here and opened the same
business?" Tyler did that smart-ass mouth thing
again.

"Yeah. Fathers and sons. Funny things, aren't
we?"

A moment passed, then I asked, "What about
your family? Are they still down in Florida?"

Tyler hesitated, then nodded. "My dad and stepmom live in Pensacola, where I grew up. He's a high
school football coach."

"Any brothers or sisters?"

"One stepsister, Bethany."

Tyler had been so open and chatty before; but
now, asking about his family, every question felt like
I was pulling answers out of him. I watched him a
moment as he fixated on our dogs.

"Are you close?"

"Huh?" He turned toward me.

"With your family? Are you close?"

"My dad's a ball buster, always has been. He raised me like I was one of his players, pushing me to work harder or be the best. I guess he's proud of me, deep down, but I always wondered if he drove me that hard for some other reason, like he could work the gay out of me or something. Let's just say he's not a big fan of the rainbow flag." He chuckled wistfully. "My stepmom's a saint, putting up with his crusty ass. I was in high school when they got married and had a rough time adjusting, but we became great friends after a couple years. She's a special woman."

"And Bethany?"

"Ah, Beth. She's . . . great."

There was something in his eyes when he said her name. He lost himself in thought or distant memories so long I thought he wasn't going to say more.

"She's fourteen, but has the intelligence of a five-year-old." His eyes drifted, and his voice became quiet. "She's the sweetest girl in the world. She just doesn't ... I don't think I've ever seen her without a smile."

He swallowed hard, and I squeezed his forearm with my hand that still rested there.

The dogs raced up and Audie stood with her paws on the fence. I reached out and scratched her ear.

I turned to catch ". . . all serious" cross Tyler's lips. "Serious?"

"Yeah. Guess it is."

It took a second, then it clicked. "It's all good. Thanks for telling me."

"Hey, you hungry?" he asked, a spark returning to his eyes.

"Yeah, starving. Want to leave Dom here while we go get something to eat? Devin and Tamara will be here to watch them."

"Sounds great."

Twenty minutes later, we sat across a table from each other in a booth at Chili's.

"Well, hello there," our twenty-something waitress said, as she flicked a lock of blonde hair behind her ear. She gaped at Tyler like he was a steak on the menu. "I'm Shauna, and I'm here to get you whatever you need."

Even I could hear the innuendo in her voice—and I was deaf!

"Uh, hi," I said. She turned toward me and, I swear, there was annoyance in her eyes. "I'd like an unsweetened iced tea, please. And can we get some chips and salsa?"

"Sure." She stared a moment after I ordered, as if considering, then turned and took a step closer to Tyler's side. "And what can I get you, handsome?"

Tyler flashed a brilliant smile. "Unsweetened iced tea too. Thanks, Shauna."

She flushed at his use of her name, then flitted away.

"God, do women do that wherever you go? Jon Snow's mom nearly licked you with her eyes."

His grin widened. "Jealous much?"

"I'm not . . . wait . . . no. I was just . . . never mind."

He laughed as I stammered. "Yeah, I get that some, but don't worry. She's not my type."

His grin morphed beyond playful into something more primal. My eyes widened, then darted to the menu. A heartbeat later, I glanced above it to find him watching me, his smirk still firmly in place. He was blazing hot, knew it, and enjoyed wielding it like a weapon—and for some reason, I found it irresistible.

Great. Just great.

"Can you teach me some signs?"

I nearly dropped my menu. "You want me to teach you ASL? Right here? In Chili's?"

"Not the whole thing. I'm a fast learner, but that might take more than one lunch." That damn smirk returned, and dammit, I nearly swooned. "Just a few signs. It looks really cool."

He thinks signing looks cool. I'm not sure if that's weird or amazing.

"Oh, I meant to ask the other day, do they mean anything? I mean, I know they're words, but do the gestures come from anything?"

I thought a moment, then held one hand to my forehead and motioned like I was gripping the bill of a baseball cap. "That's the sign for *boy*. Can you see me gripping a baseball cap?"

He mirrored my sign. "Yeah. I see it."

I then ran my thumb down my cheek. "That's *girl*."

Again, he mirrored my gesture. "What's that from?"

"The string on a girl's bonnet."

"ASL went old–school on that one. So cool."

I chuckled. "Guess so."

Shauna arrived and placed our drinks and chips on the table, then turned to me and placed a hand on my shoulder. "Honey, I'm so sorry. I didn't know you were deaf. Do you need anything?" She exaggerated her words, and I was sure she was shouting. Diners at several surrounding tables and booths turned to watch the interaction.

"I'm good. Thanks," I mumbled. She nodded and moved on to her next table.

I looked up to find Tyler's eyes fixed on the table-top.

"Hey."

His head rose.

"It's okay. I'm used to it. People mean well, they just don't know what to do."

Something in his face hardened, and "I'm sorry" was all he said.

We munched on chips and salsa quietly for a few minutes. I could see thoughts bouncing around in his head as he reached for each chip. This was our first time out, and he'd already seen *the treatment,* as Luc liked to call it.

"So," I finally broke our silence. "How do you like being a mechanic?"

"It's okay. I like working with my hands, fixing things. Sam—he's my boss—is like a brother. Working with people you like makes a big differ-ence."

"That's for sure. Tam's the sister I never had."

Our food arrived and we each dove in, un-sure how to recover the easy conversation Shauna had interrupted with her good intentions. Midway through my shrimp tacos, Tyler wiggled his fingers so I would look up.

"How do you do it?"

I cocked my head. "Do what?"

"Deal with people staring like that?"

I chuckled. "Between the two of us, I'm pretty sure you get more stares."

He rolled his eyes. "That's not the same."

"No, it's not." I set my taco down. "I don't know. I guess you just get used to it. Most people don't have anything to do with the deaf community, so we stand out. We're different. I don't take it as anything more than curiosity."

He sat back. "Huh."

"The pity is what gets to me."

"Pity?"

I nodded. "Yeah. Like there's something wrong or I'm broken somehow. I can't hear, but I'm not dumb. My friends aren't dumb either, but some of them have never heard the words they're trying to form, and that makes some people think they're slow or stupid. I get it, I guess, but it really pisses me off."

Tyler was quiet. He didn't reach for his drink or pick up his fork. He just sat there and stared. It felt like he was staring through me.

I finished the last of my taco and washed it down. He still hadn't moved or spoken.

"You okay in there?" I tried to smile.

"Oh, yeah, sorry." His eyes cleared, as though I'd woken him from some dream. "Guess I'd never . . . I mean . . . shit. I'm sorry, Gabe. This is all new to me."

My heart sank. I'd heard that line too many times to count. It was the sound of my deafness landing squarely on someone's shoulders.

My eyes drifted to my empty plate.

A second passed, then five.

Then Tyler's fingers pressed into my chin and lifted my gaze to his.

"Gabe, I don't know how to say this . . ."

Well, crap. Here it comes.

"I'm probably going to suck at being your friend because I don't know anything about being deaf. Before you, I'd never met a deaf person." He released my chin as he struggled for words. "I guess, all I know is . . . shit. If you'll be patient with me, I'd like to learn how to be a good friend."

That wasn't the next line in the script.

My mouth opened, then snapped shut.

He didn't want to run away.

He wanted *me* to be patient with *him*? My whole life had been a lesson in patience, repeating myself when hearing people didn't understand—or any of a million other things I've had to do to fit into a world I couldn't hear.

Never once had someone asked for *my* patience.

My eyes were fixed on Tyler, but my brain-to-mouth connection failed. I wanted to believe him, to believe he wanted to know more, to know *me*. I wanted to believe he'd be different and stick around.

"Is that okay?" he asked.

I didn't trust my voice, so I just nodded.

He smiled and blew out a breath I hadn't noticed he'd been holding. His eyes darted away, then back to mine as his smile widened. "In that case, you should call me Ty. That's what my closest friends call me."

Chapter 12

TYLER

My flight was scheduled for one o'clock. There'd been enough on the news about travel issues and long TSA lines lately that I knew to arrive a full two hours early. The security line was pleasantly quick, and I soon found myself sitting on a bar stool, sipping sake, at Hissho Sushi as a man in a tall white hat prepared my lunch. If all went well, I'd land in Miami around five o'clock, with plenty of time to check into my hotel and take a disco nap. This was my fourth circuit party of the year and promised to be one of the hottest.

Midway through my Pokémon roll, my phone buzzed.

SAM: DUDE. YOU FUCKED UP YET?

ME: I'm in the Nashville Airport.

SAM: You're an overachiever . . . and you didn't answer the question.

ME: Ha. No, I'm positively clear-headed. What's up?

SAM: Nothing. Miguel made me promise to give you shit about doing all that stuff down there. You know, the shit he'd put you in cuffs for.

ME: Last I recall, he put you in cuffs without you doing anything . . . and you liked it.

SAM: That's the night I learned how long his tongue really is.

ME: Eww. Mom, stop. I'll never see Dad the same way again.

SAM: Fucker. I'm your daddy. Miguel's a distant aunt at best.

ME: If you say so, MOM!

SAM: Gotta jet. When Miguel asks, tell him I screamed and shouted something really dramatic. He likes it when I'm all tough.

ME: La, la, la. Not listening. Not wanting to hear about you and Aunty Miguel and your deviant ways.

SAM: LOL fuck off . . . and have fun this weekend. Try not to be a complete idiot.

ME: I'M AN IDIOT, BUT RARELY COMPLETE. WAIT, THAT SOUNDED BAD.

SAM: NO. IT SOUNDED ABOUT RIGHT. SEE YA.

I'd barely set my phone down and reached for my chopsticks when it buzzed again.

Miguel must've really given him shit. Sheesh.

My Pokémon roll and I had a momentary staring contest, and I almost ignored the text, but Sam's shit about me being a bad texter rang in my head. He hadn't been wrong. I really needed to be better at communicating, especially with my bestie.

I glanced at the screen, but the name in the popup wasn't Sam or Miguel. It was Gabe.

The chopsticks clinked against the plate as I grabbed my phone and chuckled at the memory aid I'd used when I'd first put his number into my contacts. He hadn't given me his name then, only a note from Audie to Dom. I entered the first thing I remembered when seeing him at the coffee shop.

DEAF DIMPLES: AUDIE WANTED TO TELL DOMINO SHE HAD A GREAT TIME YESTERDAY. SHE HASN'T STOPPED TALKING ABOUT HIS BUTT. I THINK SHE HAS A CRUSH.

ME: AWW. IS IT PUPPY LOVE?

DEAF DIMPLES: THE JUDGES ARE UNANIMOUS. NO POINTS. EVEN THE RUSSIAN JUDGE PENALIZED YOUR LAMENESS, DAD.

ME: OUCH. CALLING OUT MY DAD JOKES ALREADY? TOUGH CROWD.

DEAF DIMPLES: I'M SORRY, I DIDN'T HEAR THAT. WHAT?

ME: OH, REALLY? I MAKE A LAME DOG JOKE AND GET BUSTED, BUT YOU GET TO MAKE A FAR WORSE DEAF JOKE?

DEAF DIMPLES: MY JOKE WAS ADA COMPLIANT. YOURS WAS JUST LAME.

The sushi chef glanced up as a laugh escaped me. "Sorry," I said, waving at him with my phone. He grinned, waved his knife, and resumed cutting whatever fish he'd been working on.

ME: YOU'RE GETTING ME IN TROUBLE OVER HERE.

DEAF DIMPLES: OH? SAM THAT MUCH OF A HARD ASS?

ME: LORD, NO. I MEAN . . . MIGUEL SAYS HIS ASS . . . NEVER MIND. I'M AT THE AIRPORT.

DEAF DIMPLES: THE AIRPORT? WHERE ARE YOU HEADED?

ME: MIAMI. BIG PARTY WEEKEND.

There was a long enough pause that I had time to grab my chopsticks and fumble another bite into my mouth.

DEAF DIMPLES: OH, OKAY.

I never really knew how to read a text. It's one reason I avoided them as a means of communication. Sam gave me shit thinking I was lazy or slow to respond, but I really just hated cryptic messages. Gabe's two-word sentence definitely fell into that bucket.

ME: YOU DOING OKAY? ANY WEEKEND PLANS?

DEAF DIMPLES: WE'RE GOOD. I'LL PROBABLY HANG OUT WITH THE GANG TONIGHT. IT'S FRIDAY. MIGHT TAKE AUDIE BACK TO CENTENNIAL TOMORROW IF IT'S NICE.

ME: THAT SOUNDS GREAT. I'M SURE SHE'LL LOVE IT.

DEAF DIMPLES: HEY, I JUST THOUGHT OF SOMETHING. WHO'S WATCHING DOM WHILE YOU'RE GONE?

ME: HE'S OVER AT SAM AND MIGUEL'S HOUSE. MIGUEL'S BEEN HARPING ON SAM TO GET A DOG, BUT HE DOESN'T WANT ONE. THIS GIVES M HIS FIX WITHOUT A COMMITMENT.

There was another long pause before the dots danced again.

DEAF DIMPLES: WELL, HAVE FUN THIS WEEKEND. YELL AT ME WHEN YOU GET BACK. WE CAN PLAN ANOTHER PLAY DATE FOR THE PUPS.

ME: SOUNDS GREAT. TALK SOON.

The dots danced, then stopped. They danced again, then froze. Then ... nothing.

Something about that blank screen bothered me. I finished my roll, but kept glancing back at the screen to see if a text had somehow gotten stuck in the mystical ether of cell land . . . or whatever it's called . . . but nothing came through.

The speaker above my head crackled with an announcement about my flight, so I shoved my phone into my pocket, closed out my lunch check, and headed to the gate. My gaydar clocked two other guys headed in the same direction. Each wore a stringy tank top and silky shorts that allowed their impressive equipment to flop freely. My brain spun as it switched gears into Miami mode.

Chapter 13

GABE

The group was smaller than usual. Lucas sat in his favorite spot against the wall and in–sisted I sit beside him. Bryan settled into the chair on my other side. Kevin and a couple other guys were clumped together signing on the other side.

We normally had ten or more, including a few girls. Before I could ask Luc if there was something going on, a motion at the door caught my eye. I was surprised to see Devin enter the shop and head our way. I'd invited him more times than I could count, but he'd always had some excuse. He'd always been pretty shy, preferring the company of dogs, so I'd just assumed he wasn't comfortable meeting a new group. His face lit up when our eyes met, and my sour mood brightened slightly.

Bryan gripped my arm, then made me turn so I could watch him sign while his back was to the group, his not-so-subtle version of whispering. "He's cute. Where have you been hiding him?"

I looked up to make sure Bryan was talking about the same Devin. He stood a few inches shorter than me, which put him around five seven. His muddy brown hair looked like it was parted with a grout tool and plastered to his head. He'd drawn the short straw in the Usher syndrome pool. His eyesight hadn't degenerated as quickly as his hearing, but his vision dimmed slightly with each year that passed. He had to push his thick, black-rimmed spectacles back up his nose several times before reaching the counter. Despite it all, Devin was one of the most positive, happy people I'd ever met.

I'd never thought of him as cute, but in a nerdy, endearing way, it was there.

"Who? Devin? He works at my academy."

"Gabriel Rossi, have you been hiding an office romance from me?"

I rolled my eyes. "First, I don't work in an office. Second, absolutely not. Devin's sweet and all, but no. Just no."

He glanced over his shoulder at Devin as he stood in line for coffee.

"So I'm free to hunt? He's fair game?"

"If you think you can wrangle that cat, go for it. He's pretty shy though, and you're . . . well . . . you."

"What's that supposed to mean?" He pooched out his lip in an exaggerated pout.

"Let's just say you're more, um, *outgoing* than he is. Just be gentle with Bambi, okay?"

His pout turned into a wide grin and clapped his fingertips together several times before signing, "Bambi. I love it. That'll be my pet name for him."

"Bry, why are we friends? Can you remind me?"

"Because I'm fabulous, and you couldn't live without me." His outward-facing palms practically set the air on fire as he signed *fabulous*. The last thing I wanted to do was encourage him, but a laugh slipped out.

He blew me a kiss to punctuate his point.

As we turned back toward the group, Devin nudged his way from the counter to our circle, then stood just outside and glanced from one person to the next. Bryan started to move, but I clamped a hand on his arm and held him down, then signed, "You'll scare the poor thing away. Move over a seat. I'll go get him."

"You're so bossy. It kind of turns me on."

I pinched the bridge of my nose, then rose and crossed the ring.

"Hey, Devin. Glad you could make it," I signed. Bryan had been right: his nervous smile was pretty cute.

"Thanks. The group's smaller than I expected." Relief washed across his face.

I nodded. "We're missing a few tonight. Come on, I'll introduce you to everyone."

We made our way around the circle, me introducing Devin and him struggling to make eye contact with each new person he met. I felt for him, but couldn't stop a snort from escaping when Bryan stuck his thumbs to his temples with his other fingers spread wide in the sign for *deer*. Thankfully, Devin was too frightened by his social shadow to see anything around him.

Twenty minutes later, as Lucas was holding court, lecturing the group about some upcoming event at the school, my eyes drifted toward the door where my mind saw Tyler stand and wave. His hair fell about his shoulders and fluttered as the door opened, and his eyes glittered like gems.

A shuffle next to me brought me back to the present. I turned to find Bryan had swapped seats with Devin. Poor Bambi sat with his ankles crossed beneath his chair and his arms folded.

"What's with you?" Bryan signed as discreetly as was possible in a circle of men who could see everything.

"What are you talking about?"

He raised a brow. "You're not here. Your body is, but *you* are somewhere else—and by the look on your face, it isn't somewhere good. Are you okay?"

"I'm fine. Can we just listen to Luc?" I tried to turn, but his hand grabbed my arm.

"Is it that guy? The dog guy?"

"He's not a dog guy . . . I mean, he is. He has a dog. Can we talk about this later?"

He eyed me a second. "Fine. But we're not done. Mama Bry is here to listen and advise."

"Dear god, I'm screwed."

He slapped my arm.

Luc stopped signing and the entire circle glared. For the first time that night, I wanted to shrink under my chair more than Bambi.

Devin ended up in the corner of the shop with Kevin, our resident Dungeons and Dragons player. I'd encouraged Devin to join us because I thought he could use the support of the group. Setting him up was never in my mind; but seeing the gathering of geeks whose names actually rhymed made it all worthwhile. Their signs were animated, and their eyes never drifted from each other.

"There's so much electricity over there I think I felt a shock," Bryan signed with a humorless pucker on his lips.

"Aww, did our resident hunter let Bambi slip through his net?"

"Have you heard them? They're comparing stats or something. I can feel the *fabulous* falling off me as we stand here. Please, get me out of this place."

He hooked his arm around mine and dragged me toward the door as I tried to say goodbye to Lucas. He quirked a brow when I mouthed "Help me!" but wasn't quick enough to save me from being dragged into the parking lot.

When we got to Bryan's car, he unhooked our arms and faced me. "Now, out with it. What happened?"

Good grief. He's a dog with a bone.

"Nothing happened. Everything's fine."

He turned the *okay* sign upside down: "Asshole."

"Hey—"

"Come on, you've been mopey all night. Let's go get a real drink. Maybe that'll loosen you up enough to tell me what's crawled up your ass."

I loved Bry like a brother, but asking advice from him felt like getting nutritional guidance from a Pez dispenser.

The drink, on the other hand, offered solid guidance, so I nodded.

"Can we just go around the corner to Olive Garden? I'd rather not go to a bar."

"Sure. Race you there."

Five minutes later, we sat in the bar section of our favorite breadsticks–and–salad eatery with two glasses of red wine sitting before us threatening to spill over the rim. The bartender winked as Bry carefully raised his glass and took a sip without spilling a drop.

I tried, but dribbled a trail of vino all over the bar.

"That's alcohol abuse," Bryan teased. "Use your straw to suck it up."

I scrunched up my face. "You're disgusting. *You* suck it up."

"You'd like that, wouldn't you?"

God, I fell for his trap. He laughed, and the damn bartender chuckled too.

"Drink your juice and start talking." Bryan strummed his fingers on the rim of his glass and watched me closely.

I sat back and hung my head. "Bry, nothing happened, really. Ty's just out of town this weekend."

"Ty?"

"Tyler, the mechanic."

He grinned. "I know who you're talking about. You're using a nickname now. It's cute."

"Shut up. He told me to call him Ty, said it's what his close friends call him."

"So you're close now?"

"Friends. Close *friends*. He was very clear on that."

Bryan leaned back. "Oh. I get it now.

"You get what?"

"He put you in the friend zone, and you don't like it."

"Bry . . ." I started, then stopped. "I . . . maybe. I guess. We really had fun though. Everything felt so good."

"Did he kiss you?"

"No."

"Did he try?"

"No. We were never anywhere private though."

Bryan cocked a brow. "I'm sorry, but if I want to kiss a guy, I find a time and place."

"Maybe," was all I could think to say as I grabbed my wine and swallowed half the glass. I stared into the ruby liquid for a long moment before I realized Bry's fingers were flying.

"Where's he going?"

"What?"

"You said he was going out of town. Where's he going?"

"Miami. To a circuit party."

Bryan grimaced, but didn't say anything.

"I feel stupid even thinking about it. He's just a guy I've met a couple times. We haven't even been on a real date."

"He came to the academy and took you to lunch. That's a date, even if you didn't get any lip action."

"I guess. He's so far out of my league. I know that, but I really like this guy, Bry."

"Out of your league? Stop that." Bryan scowled again. "How's he been with the whole deaf thing?"

I thought a moment. "He said he'd never dated a deaf guy, said he'd never even met one."

"Gabe—"

"I know." I didn't mean to slam my fingers into my forehead, but my heart was twisting in my chest. I closed my eyes and breathed in a few times to calm myself. "I know what you're going to say—the same thing Luc would say—but he's different. We've talked about it some, and he hasn't run away."

Bryan stared into the coffee shop a moment, then signed, "So what's got you so upset? Him calling you a friend? The party?"

"No, it's not that. Well, maybe a little. I don't know. Does that mean he's into drugs and all that? I don't even know what to think, Bry." I turned away, then back. "I've never dated somebody into all that stuff. I don't even like to go to local bars, much less fly around the country to party."

Bryan sat quietly and sipped his drink. His silence was more unnerving than his constant stream of questions.

He finally set his empty glass down and signed, "You really like this one, don't you?"

I glanced up and nodded.

He shook his head and a tight smile formed. "Whatever you do, do not text him this weekend, okay?"

I nodded again, thinking that was exactly what I wanted to do once we left the restaurant.

But I knew Bry was right. Even if he responded, the Tyler I knew wouldn't be the guy texting back. That thought made my heart sink further.

Chapter 14

TYLER

Friday night was insane. Studio Sixty hosted the weekend's opening party featuring Israeli DJ Orel Sabag. I'd been to dozens of parties and clubs, but had never heard such hard-hitting Brazilian beats mixed with high-energy vocals. The whole place was decorated like a jungle, and lasers firing from every corner of the ceiling cast images of dangling fruits and wild animals above our heads. A few times we actually ducked as a virtual ape or leopard dove from their rooftop perch. Each new song brought an onslaught of visual sensations that drove the sweaty, shirtless sea of chemically induced men into a frenzy.

The Miami sun poking through the skylight in my Airbnb roused me on Saturday morning. A hairy, muscular arm was wrapped around my waist, and my lower half was tangled between a pair of equally furry legs. I carefully unwound myself and sat on the bed's edge, glancing back to find the cherry of my Friday night's sundae still sound asleep.

Pedro? Paulo? No, Pachu. Right. That's his name. I'm almost sure.

It didn't really matter. He was beyond hot, and Argentinian, which meant the sex had been off the charts. We'd wake, shower, and go our separate ways, likely to never see each other again—and that's how the single circuit party gods intended it.

I padded into the bathroom and started the shower. By the time I was toweling off, Pachu was squeezing back into his jeans. I shook my head and gave him a blank stare when he said something in Spanish, then remembered he didn't speak a word of English.

Unable to recall the English word for "good-bye," he waved, then turned and left. I stared after him a moment, the haze of the prior night's festivities still clouding my mind. Something in that odd exchange felt so familiar.

Then it hit me.

It was the wave.

He'd waved just like Gabe had that first night we'd met. Floppy brown hair and dimples suddenly flared in my mind, and I couldn't suppress a smile. I briefly wondered what he was up to this weekend, then my stomach rumbled and thoughts of pancakes and sausage replaced his grin. Unlike some guys I knew who partook in substances that killed one's appetite, I stuck to the ones that lit my fire without stealing my desire to eat everything in sight, so I threw on some shorts and a flimsy tank and headed out to find breakfast.

It was past noon by the time I'd risen from the dead, and breakfast was hard to come by. The IHOP and Denny's within walking distance were both packed, with lines out the door, so I opted for a street vendor's chorizo and chicken burrito instead. The next few hours were spent lounging on the beach, watching one magazine cover after another pass by. I wasn't sure at what point one became numb to sheer perfection, but I'd never quite reached it, and my head snapped back and forth so quickly I was sure I'd need a chiropractor after this trip.

I'd finally drifted off when my phone buzzed.

SAM: YOU ALIVE. MOTHER'S ASKING.

ME: WOULD YOU TELL MIGUEL TO GET OFF MY ASS. HE'S RIDING ME SO HARD WE MIGHT NEED A PREGNANCY TEST SOON.

SAM: HA HA. HE WOULDN'T DARE. BEST YOU'LL GET OUT OF US IS BECOMING AN UNCLE.

ME: WAIT. ARE YOU TWO TRYING TO GET PREGGERS? YOU KNOW THAT WON'T WORK, RIGHT?

SAM: I THINK I LIKED YOU BETTER WHEN YOU WERE AFRAID I'D FIRE YOU.

ME: YOU COULD NEVER FIRE ME. YOUR SHOP WOULD FALL APART. BESIDES, YOU LOVE ME AND YOU KNOW IT.

Sam: I will admit to liking you on occasion. That's all you get. I'll let Miguel know you haven't croaked yet.

Sam: Stay safe, okay? I wouldn't care, but M would be a mess if anything happened to you.

I stared at the screen a long moment. Setting aside Sam's usual layers of sarcasm, there was genuine concern hidden in plain sight of that text. Hell, it wasn't even hidden. Sam had never said anything like that. I'd never considered myself a softie, or even the deep end of an emotional kiddie pool, but I couldn't stop reading that text.

Sam: You still there?

Me: Yeah, sorry. Just got distracted.

Me: Give Dom a scratch for me. I'll be good. Oh, and give Mom my love.

SAM: I'LL GIVE HIM A SLOBBERY KISS FOR YOU. I KNOW THAT'S HOW YOU LIKE IT.

ME: THIS NUMBER IS NO LONGER IN SERVICE. PLEASE HANG UP AND TRY AGAIN.

SAM: THAT JOKE ONLY WORKS FOR A PHONE CALL, ASSWIPE. GO HAVE FUN AND BE SAFE. PEACE OUT.

I tossed my phone aside and shut my eyes. An hour later, my skin was sizzling, and my phone's alarm chirped, reminding me to get ready for the next party.

Saturday afternoon featured a pool party at one of the large resort-style hotels that overlooked the ocean. From the drink stands lining either side of the hotel's automatic glass doors, all the way to the rolling ocean's edge, there was barely room to move without rubbing against nearly naked men in thongs and trunks.

Three hours into the party, I found myself in an elevator headed up to a suite on the fourteenth floor with six guys from California. We passed each other back and forth more times than a desperate pro football team shuffling the ball about on the last play of a game.

By eight o'clock, I'd had a quick dinner at a corner diner, finally satisfying my craving for breakfast food, and was lying in bed for the mid-weekend disco nap. The Saturday night party was considered the main event, and I wanted to be well rested.

The Cali boys had sucked the life out of me. Literally.

Chapter 15

TYLER

"Have I mentioned that Mondays suck?"

Sam grinned as he sipped his coffee. "Only every Monday since I've known you. Assume there are fifty-two Mondays each year, times the eight years we've been friends, that's over four hundred times you've reminded me how much you love Mondays."

I groaned and pressed the button on his Keurig, willing it to give me strength. "I hate you sometimes. You're a miserable asshole."

He chuckled. "From what I can see, you're the miserable one. And after this weekend, I bet your asshole—"

"Please don't make me sit or ride the cart under the cars today. It hurts to walk too fast."

"What time did you get in yesterday?"

"My flight was scheduled for three, but got delayed due to weather. I guess the rain yesterday was a good thing. It kept me from baking on the beach again."

"How was the party?"

"Parties. There was one each night, and one during the day on Saturday and Sunday. I blew off the tea dance Sunday to come home though."

Sam shook his head. "If Miguel and I go out for one drink, I'm hurting the next day. I can't imagine all those parties in one weekend."

"Yeah, but you two are old and crusty." I saluted with my mug. "Saturday night was the best one ever. There had to be thousands of guys crammed onto the beach. The dance floor was under these pink and white tarps that stretched for a solid hundred yards, and there still wasn't room for all the guys under there. There must've been at least fifty disco balls hanging from the scaffolding. The guys made a game out of counting them. It was nuts."

"Meet anybody? It seems so strange to go to something like that alone."

"Not strange at all. And yes, I met a lot of people. You should've seen the guy I left the party with Sunday morning. His name was Blake. Or Barry. I can't remember. He's an accountant from Boston who also competes in amateur bodybuilding competitions. The term 'nerdy hot' was invented for this guy."

"Did you test his stamina?"

I chuckled. "He had a lot of it to test. Huge stamina, actually, way more than I would've expected from a pumped-up muscle head."

"I get the image." Sam held up his palms as he rolled his eyes. Then he cocked his head and asked, "What's that look? You just got serious all of a sudden."

"I don't know. It's probably nothing."

"Tyler Hyatt. No secrets. Out with it."

I stared into my coffee a second. "Sunday morning, I woke up to Blake mumbling in his sleep. He was curled up in the fetal position and pressed as close against my body as he could get. My arms were wrapped around him, and he was holding them in place with his hands. I guess we slept like that all night."

"Okay. I'm not getting what's wrong with this picture."

"I don't know, Sam. I watched him sleep for a minute. All his bravado from the night before was gone, and it was just this guy cradled in my arms, dreaming about who knows what. I wasn't thinking or anything. I just leaned down and kissed his nose … and that's when he woke up."

"Sounds like a shred of humanity peeking out. Go on."

"He glanced up and said, 'Hey, you.'"

Sam waited. When I didn't continue, he cocked his head and asked, "That's it? That's the big event that has you turning pensive?"

"I don't know what pensive means, Sam, but yeah, it made me think."

Sam chuckled.

"I mean, he was smiling when he said it, and his eyes . . . fuck, Sam. It all felt so . . . like something. Circuit parties aren't supposed to give me feelings. They damn sure aren't supposed to make me want to cuddle."

"Ty, I'm still not getting why any of this is bad. Did you get the guy's number?"

"Hell no. I'm not interested in some guy who lives a thousand miles away. I don't even want to date. I'm happy. Dom and I are happy."

Sam eyed me a moment. I felt my skin crawl under his gaze. He really would make a good father one day.

"Why do I get the feeling that's not everything? What have you left out?"

"Are you fucking psychic?"

He shrugged. "I know you. Now, what else is bothering you? Did you feel some other basic human emotion that has your panties in a wad?"

I flicked him the bird.

"When Blake got up to shower, I didn't. I just laid there. My hand wandered over to where he'd been, to feel the warmth or whatever. All of a sudden, I felt . . . empty, or shallow . . . like there was a hole inside me and I was falling into it."

When Sam didn't make a smart-ass remark, I chanced a glance. His eyes were knitted together.

"My god, this is serious," he finally said.

"What?" I leaned forward.

"You might actually have a heart under all that bullshit."

"I've told you I hate you, right?"

He laughed again, then stood. "I gotta get started. We've got a full lineup today. When your two remaining brain cells start rubbing together, come out and I'll give you a work order."

"One more cup. Give me ten minutes."

"Fine," he called out as the door shut behind him.

I sat and stared into my coffee for a minute longer, then added another Splenda. Photos blanketed the far wall of Sam's office where the coffee cart sat. My eyes roamed from one smiling client to the next. One leaned against the front of a Buick, another waved from the driver's seat of a Ford.

There were a few images of Miguel and Donna, his partner, each sporting their navy uniform. They were an odd couple. Miguel towered over most men, and Donna was a petite woman. Side by side, they were almost comical, especially in uniform.

I was surprised to find a picture of Sam, Miguel, and me. I didn't recognize the field, but Domino was there, running circles around us, no doubt wishing one of us would throw a ball or run so he could play chase. Miguel's hand rested casually on Sam's shoulder. They were rarely together without one touching the other. I'd never given it much thought, but that photo—and whatever mood had struck following the night with Blake—drew me in.

Then I stared at Domino. His lopsided grin and goofy tongue made me smile. I'd never loved anyone like I loved that furry beast. Something inside me swelled as I thought of him greeting me last night after a weekend apart. Miguel and Sam had nothing on sticking to each other's side when compared to Dom and me.

I turned away from the photo wall and downed the last of my coffee, intending to get the day started so I could take Dom to the dog park before it got dark. My phone lit up and unlocked when I grabbed it and looked down. I'm not sure what sequence of butt-dialing occurred, but the last text exchange I'd had with Gabe was on the screen.

Without thinking, I typed:

ME: HEY, YOU.

Chapter 16

GABE

"We're already up to twenty, and more cars are pulling up." There was near-mania on her face as she spoke.

On our best day, we'd babysat eighteen pups in one day, and that was a stretch. The pen was large enough to handle that many, but with large and small dogs mixed together, refereeing the inevitable scuffles became a challenge for one person. Devin was only part-time and rarely worked Mondays, which meant it was just Tamara and me—and I had three training appointments that would pull me away from the pack for an hour at a time.

"We really need to add a fence and section off the small dogs into their own pen," she said.

I nodded absently, dreading the thought of stealing running room from the larger breeds.

"Guess that flyer we left at the dog park really worked. I'm scared of what the promo with the vets will do when it hits next month," I said. "I'll look at it when we get done here. Maybe there's room to create a small-dog pen on the side without chopping up the main yard."

"You might need to get Dev to start coming in full-time too."

I nodded. That would be a lot more difficult than building a fence. Devin laid down the law about only working part-time when he joined us a couple years ago. He'd probably want more money than I could afford. I scribbled a note on the desk pad to check with the local colleges and vet schools for students who wanted part-time work.

A woman with two schnauzers entered, making our total for the day twenty-two. Her two wiry mates barked like mad when a man and his Great Dane crossed the threshold a few steps behind them. The Dane merely looked bored and barely glanced their way. I turned back to find Audie watching all three with keen interest.

Twenty minutes and five dogs later, our total nearly hit thirty and Tam was busy chasing fur balls and wiggle butts in the main pen. I had a brief moment of peace before my ten o'clock training appointment arrived, so I decided to call the fence company and get that project on the books. My cell was already flashing when I picked it up.

DOM'S DAD: HEY, YOU.

Unlike most of my weekend, I'd made it through the morning without thinking about Tyler. I hadn't really expected him to reach out while he was in Miami, but a tiny voice in my head kept urging me to check my phone every hour, just in case. That little voice is a terrorist and should be put on some watch list.

I stared at the message a long moment, a silly grin crawling across my face, before typing a response worthy of a Shakespearean sonnet.

ME: HEY.

The dots didn't dance in response. I waited a solid three minutes, even pretended to look for the fence company's phone number in a notebook I knew didn't contain it, then turned back to my phone and stared. Nada.

He's probably under a car.

Like he was under some guy this weekend, that tiny terrorist in my head echoed.

Shut up. He's a grown man—and we're just friends.

Fuck. I was responding to my internal voice. This was bad.

I closed the texting app and opened my contacts to scroll for the fence company, desperate to get my mind off Tyler and whatever—or whoever—he'd done this weekend. I knew it was silly to be jealous. We'd only seen each other a few times, and he wasn't mine. I didn't really even know him.

Why did logic have to make so much sense when my heart wanted to find meaning where there was none?

One fence conversation later, I had an appointment for a guy to come out, measure, and give me an estimate. The light on my phone had flashed during the call, but I ignored it—barely. As soon as the fence guy said "See you then," my fingers flew to open the text app again.

DOM'S DAD: YOU HAVE A GOOD WEEKEND?
DO ANYTHING FUN WITH YOUR LADY?

A normal conversation. He was starting a normal conversation like he hadn't just gone out of town to a wild, orgy-filled drug fest. Anger flared as I glared at the screen. Then my rational brain bitch-slapped me back into reality and I grinned at Ty wanting to talk to me again.

ME: LADY? I DON'T THINK ANYONE IN THE HISTORY OF DOGS HAS EVER CALLED A HUNDRED TWENTY POUND GERMAN SHEPHERD A LADY.

DOM'S DAD: OKAY, SO SHE'S A PRETTY BUTCH LADY, BUT EVEN THE MOST DIE-HARD HOME DEPOT DYKES DESERVE TO BE LADIES TOO, WHEN THEY WANT TO BE.

ME: LOL YOU'RE AN IDIOT, YOU KNOW THAT?

DOM'S DAD: SO SAM TELLS ME EVERY DAY AT WORK.

Motion pulled my gaze upward as a woman with an Australian shepherd entered.

ME: HEY, MY NEXT APPOINTMENT JUST SHOWED UP. WE'RE DROWNING TODAY. CHAT LATER?

DOM'S DAD: YOU BET.

Snickers, the caramel-and-black Aussie, was one of my more advanced students, and was a blast to work with. At eighteen months old, I estimated her vocabulary at around fifty commands, with no end in sight. Her human wanted her to learn agility training, more for the exercise than any desire to compete. She grasped most of the jumping skills quickly, but struggled on the tube, where she lost the world around her for a couple seconds, so today was dedicated to tube drills.

I grabbed my already stuffed treat pouch and led Snickers into the large pen. Tam was bent over a swirling mass of fur, pulling two mini somethings apart. She waved without glancing up as we entered the training area.

By the time the red lights strobed, Snickers had completed three successful runs through half the agility course, which included three jump sequences and the tube. She leapt into my arms, clearly proud of her own accomplishment and relishing the praise I was heaping on her. Snickers wasn't nearly as motivated by treats as she was by human affection and praise.

When we turned toward the office, I smiled at her owner, who stood just outside the fence applauding. Snickers bolted toward her with a wide smile and lolling tongue.

I gave a quick summary of our lesson and ushered the pair into the office and then the parking lot. Snickers tugged against her leash to give me one last kiss before hopping into a BMW convertible's passenger seat.

Snickers's owner got a phone call and didn't drive away. My phone buzzed about the same time.

DOM'S DAD: SO, I WAS THINKING ...

ME: DID IT HURT? YOU KNOW THAT'S DANGEROUS?

DOM'S DAD: HA HA. YOU SOUND LIKE SAM AGAIN. YOU TWO BEEN TALKING BEHIND MY BACK?

ME: NOPE. YOU'RE JUST EASY.

Shit. I just called him easy. Is he going to be offended or get mad?

DOM'S DAD: HA. I'VE BEEN CALLED EASY A TIME OR TWO. I PREFER TO THINK OF IT AS HOSPITABLE.

ME: WOW. JUST WOW.

DOM'S DAD: HEY, BEFORE SAM CRACKS THE WHIP AGAIN (AND NO, THAT WASN'T A HOSPITALITY REFERENCE), WANT TO DO THE DOG PARK WITH US TONIGHT? WE COULD GRAB DINNER AFTER. I'M NOT A CHEF OR ANYTHING, BUT I CAN GRILL A MEAN BURGER.

Of all the things he could've said, that was the last thing I'd expected. He was asking me on a date! Holy shit. Right there in my parking lot, I hopped up and down and spun around. Snickers cocked her head and barked once. Thankfully, her human was still distracted with her call.

ME: SURE. SOUNDS GREAT. I'LL FINALLY GET TO SEE YOUR LAIR.

DOM'S DAD: LAIR? YOU SOUND LIKE I'M PLANNING TO WHACK YOU OVER THE HEAD AND DRAG YOU BACK BY YOUR FEET.

ME: DON'T THREATEN ME WITH A GOOD TIME.

DOM'S DAD: LOL I'M STARTING TO THINK YOU'RE THE WEIRDO HERE. I KINDA LIKE IT. SEE YOU AT THE PARK AROUND 6:30?

ME: SEE YOU THEN.

I did another hop as the screen darkened. It took all my willpower to keep from shouting. Ms. BMW finally finished her call, revved her engine, and pulled slowly away. Snickers barked a goodbye as they drove past.

My heart felt warm for the first time in days.

Aussies had a way of doing that to me.

That was the Aussie. Sure, right, the terrorist chuckled in the background.

Chapter 17

GABE

Audie passed out in the car. She'd greeted Dom like they were long-lost litter mates reunited after years apart, prancing and spinning through excited whimpers and barks. For his part, Dom looked like he might wiggle his butt off. Tyler and I laughed long after they'd darted away to find something to sniff or some other dog to chase. We stood beneath several tall shade trees for nearly an hour and a half, chatting and watching them play.

I'd had a million conversations in my life, but couldn't remember one that flowed as easily as that one. The only time our banter slowed was when one of the dogs would slam into us for a quick check-in. This was usually followed by the other furry fiend barreling headlong into the other of us.

I'm not sure who laughed more, the dogs or their humans.

A couple times, when I'd lean over to pet one of the dogs, Tyler's hand found its way to my back. It was such a simple touch, sometimes compounded by a circular rub, but it felt like so much more. At one point, he leaned in like he was going to kiss me, and I thought I might keel over right there in the park. His hand brushed my arm, and his skin against mine sent my mind to places it only visited at night, when I was alone and far too worked up to sleep. I was just glad we stood a good distance from most of the other owners so no one else would see the embarrassing bulge in my shorts that resulted from his near-kiss.

As I watched Tyler pull into his condo complex, my pulse began pounding, and I realized I was about to walk into his home. I'd known we were eating dinner there since he invited me over, but the reality of entering his personal space hadn't set in until that moment. I glanced over to see if Audie shared my nervousness, but she only eyed me with a half-lidded disinterest.

Tyler and Dom waited outside his door as I parked, then leashed Audie and strode up. He turned to unlock the door, and I thought I felt him talking. I touched his arm and he turned as the door opened.

"... usually neater."

"What? I didn't get the first part," I said.

"Oh, sorry. I said you'll have to forgive the mess. Being out of town threw me off my cleaning game."

Dom raced inside the moment the door cracked open, and Audie tugged at her leash, determined to follow. Once she was freed and happily investigating the new environment, we walked inside.

I'm not sure what I expected from a pretty boy mechanic with a furry friend—maybe eighties posters or beanbag chairs with chewed seams—but a condo that could've been featured in *Urban Lifestyle* magazine wasn't it. We walked into an open den filled with cream-colored couches and a wide, comfy-looking leather chair. Delicate lamps cast a warm glow on either side of a massive flat-screen TV mounted on the far wall. A stacked-stone fireplace held court on the far end, its mantle crowned with elegant candlesticks and knickknacks.

"Wow. Really nice place, Ty."

He turned back, a broad smile parting his lips. "Thanks. Not what you expected, is it?"

I shook my head and finally closed my mouth. Apparently, I'd been gaping.

He shrugged. "What can I say? My mama raised me to like a nice home. Sam and Miguel give me grief about it too. That makes it worth it. Neither of them can decorate for shit."

His grin faded, and something shifted in his eyes. I stepped closer.

"What are you thinking?"

"Sorry. I lost my mom when I was twelve. I guess doing things like this reminds me of her, keeps her around somehow. Sounds silly when I say it out loud."

I rested a hand on his arm. "That's not silly at all, Ty."

He stared down at me for the longest moment. I didn't dare move my hand. I could barely breathe. Just when I thought we might stay frozen there all night, he said, "I like it when you call me Ty."

That wasn't even on the menu of what I expected him to say. My mouth opened, but didn't work. He grinned, then leaned over and kissed my cheek.

My knees wobbled as he turned and padded into the kitchen. My inner preteen took over and my hand raised itself to touch the cheek he'd just kissed, as if it could press that touch deeper into me and save it for later.

Ty waving his hands from across the kitchen island snapped my head up, as my hand dropped to my side.

"You like tater tots or french fries better? We're going healthy deep-fried tonight. Screw my diet."

"Diet? You're on a diet? Do you have *any* body fat?"

And just like that, he lifted his shirt and pinched the skin clinging to his six bronzed beauties. Sweet baby Jesus, his abs were a work of art. For the second time in as many minutes, I nearly toppled over.

"Diet's a poor word choice. Eating lifestyle is more appropriate. Tonight, we're leaping head-first off the wagon."

I just nodded, unable to trust my voice—or my balance.

"So, tots or fries?"

"Definitely tots," I said.

"Good man. I knew you had taste," he quipped, then turned and put the bag of french fries back in the freezer.

I scanned his kitchen, again surprised to find high-end pots and pans hanging on the far wall like a display case, a set of black-handled knives with Japanese characters emblazoned on the end protruding from a richly stained butcher block, and a three-tiered hanging basket laden with potatoes, onions and other fresh vegetables. When my eyes returned to Tyler, he was turned and grinning.

"Didn't peg me for a chef?"

I shook my head.

"There are layers to this cake, mister. You'll see." He winked and turned to grab an onion from the mesh basket and pull a knife from the block. I watched as he diced the onion faster than I could usually remove the peel. It was like watching one of those chef shows on TV, but not the ones with home cooks, the other ones where the pros go head-to-head. He caught me gaping and flicked a piece of onion with the tip of his knife, like Hibachi cooks do during their dinner table shows. I was so hung up on the idea that he wanted me "to see his layers" that I didn't move quick enough, and the darn thing landed right on my head.

Tyler laughed as I picked it out of my hair.

"So, you're good with knives and cars—" I started.

"Don't forget dogs. You might be a professional, but I'm a pretty good amateur dad."

I grinned. "I'll withhold judgment on that. So far, it looks like Dom is doing more of the training than his dad."

"Hey! I taught him that, thank you very much." He waved his knife in the air. "Mind getting the plates and glasses while I start the burgers? It's nice out. We can eat on the patio, if you're okay with that?"

"Sounds great," I said as I walked around the island.

When I got within a step, he leaned forward and kissed me on the lips, then stepped back and pointed as though nothing had happened. "Plates are in there. Glasses are in that cabinet." Without another word, he grabbed the plate with the hamburger patties and escaped through a sliding glass door.

I gripped the countertop as my heart danced a jig. Tyler had just kissed me ... on the mouth. Had he meant to do that? Or did he trip and catch himself with my lips? Guys did that occasionally, right? I was sure I'd seen that in a movie.

I'd spent all weekend sulking and obsessing about whatever he'd been up to in Miami—and the fact that his "whatever" hadn't included talking with me at all—but here he was, on his first day back, cooking dinner with me and tumbling into my lips.

I ran my tongue over where he'd touched them, begging for there to be saltiness or some other taste I could savor and obsess over when this night ended, but there was nothing other than my own honey–flavored lip balm. I made a mental note to get him some unique flavor so he could leave a mark next time . . .

And there I was, planning a next kiss, right there in the middle of his kitchen.

I felt the hint of a vibration that I was pretty sure hadn't come from my own heart. Tyler was knocking on the glass of the door and waving with his other hand, so I turned to face him.

"Can you hand me two slices of cheese? They're in the top of the fridge door."

I nodded numbly.

I opened a stainless steel door to discover his freakin' fridge was more organized than a college library. Every shelf contained at least two plastic organizers, some of which had organizers inside them to ensure even more perfect order. Even his apples were lined up in rows next to lemons and oranges, just like in the produce section at the grocery store. I'd never seen anything like it, not even in magazine ads for designer kitchen products.

Who did this?

The cheese was precisely where he'd said, standing neatly beside a clear box containing sticks of butter whose wax paper labels all scrawled in the same direction. I was almost afraid to touch anything for fear I might not be able to get it back in the right place. Thankfully, the cheese slices slipped out without disturbing anything else.

I slid the glass door open to find a wide patio surrounded by a wall of intricately laid stacked stone that rose a hand above my head. Several plush cushions filled black iron patio chairs at one end, while Tyler worked his magic at a monster grill at the other. Seriously, it was the mother of all grills, with three levels of racks and a whole set of four side burners for pots or whatever. As impressive as the equipment was, I couldn't find a single smudge on its chrome or bit of char or ash in the grill bed.

"Is that a new grill?" I asked as I handed him the cheese.

"No, guess I've had if for three, maybe four years now."

"And you've used it before?" I couldn't hide the wonder from my voice.

"I like to keep my things in good working order." He smirked and cocked a brow. "How do you like your meat?"

"My . . . what?" I stammered.

He barked a laugh. "Your hamburger meat. How do you like it cooked?"

My cheeks warmed. "Oh, medium, yeah. I like it medium."

His eyes twinkled when he grinned, sending a completely different flood of heat through me. I turned to flee back into the safety of the kitchen.

"I'm gonna get the plates now. And glasses. We'll need those. Right?"

I'm sure he answered, probably through another bout of laughter, but I was already turned and headed inside.

A short time later, we sat on the patio with two dogs staring intently as we took each bite.

"What did you put in these burgers? My god, they're amazing."

He beamed. "Ancient Chinese recipe."

I rolled my eyes.

"No really. Chinese five spice, some Chinese peppers, soy sauce, ginger, and a handful of other ingredients."

My brows must've hit my hairline, because he had to set his beer down to keep from spitting it across the table. "What? Didn't think I could cook?"

"I didn't think you should be in a professional kitchen, no. Seriously, Ty, this is fantastic. Is this some special burger of yours, or do you really know how to cook like this all the time?"

He looked up, then his eyes fell to his plate. I swear he was embarrassed. This sure-of-himself hottie was suddenly self-conscious. I couldn't have been more intrigued.

"You have to tell me, Ty. I'm dyin' over here."

His grin widened and he relaxed. "I might have spent some time in culinary school."

"Might? Dude, seriously? That's so cool. When? Why aren't you a famous chef?"

He chuckled. "Not sure how famous I'd be, but becoming a chef was never my goal. I just did it to keep myself sane back when . . ."

All humor drained from his face, and his eyes drifted past me for the first time that night.

I didn't know what to say, so I took another bite to give him a moment.

"I told you about losing my mom when I was twelve."

I nodded.

"That was so hard. She was . . . she was everything. I was too young to know how to grieve. Hell, I'm not sure you're ever really old enough to know that, at least not when it's your mom who dies. Her cancer was awful. We watched her fade from the most vibrant woman in the world into a shell of her former self. When we finally lost her, my dad . . ."

His throat caught, and moisture formed around the edges of his eyes. He grabbed his beer and took a long sip, probably more to gather himself than anything. I glanced down to find Dom resting his head in Tyler's lap, no doubt sensing his change in mood. Ty's hand absently stroked his fur.

"I thought we were going to lose my dad too." A tear finally escaped and rolled down his cheek. "They'd known each other since elementary school."

I watched him take a few deep breaths and wipe the tear away. "He picked on her all the way through middle school. She hated him, until their junior year of high school. Depending on which of them told the story, either he saved her from drowning or she pushed him into a pool. Either way, that night sparked something special that turned into a lifetime love affair. Watching her slip away, caring for her as the light of her eyes dimmed . . . something died inside him too."

"Ty, I'm so sorry."

He sipped his beer in silence for a long moment, taking comfort in Domino's companionship.

"It took a long time for both of us to, I don't know, to just be okay. Six years later, he met a really great woman. A year after that, they married.""Were you okay with that?"

Ty stared into the distance a moment before answering. "When they first started dating, Dad kept it a secret. At least, he tried to. I knew something was up almost immediately. He never dressed up before, especially after Mom . . . When he came home late one night wearing slacks and a pressed shirt—and smelling like perfume—the cat was out of the bag. I think I was more pissed that he'd kept it from me than anything. We never kept secrets."

He finished his beer and tossed the bottle into a bin near the sliding door.

"Dana—that's my stepmom—is amazing. She became part of the family the day she walked in the door that first time, and there was something in that relationship that healed more than just my dad's heart. I think it pulled mine together too."

"How so?"

"I was pretty angry after Mom died. I was twelve turning twenty—at least, that's what I thought. I was always bigger than other kids, so being angry all the time wasn't a good thing for anyone. I spent most of my high school years wanting to punch somebody for no good reason—and never under-standing why. I was trying to grow up, dealing with the gap left by my mom's death, and struggling to understand the hormones and evolving sexuality flowing through my veins. I played basketball, so I was surrounded by friends and teammates. I was popular. And yet, somehow, I felt so alone. I still feel like that sometimes."

I barely knew what to say. Tyler had opened up more in one conversation than some of my friends had in years. I'd been attracted to him from the moment our eyes met in the coffee shop, but after his weekend in Miami, I was starting to think Bryan was right, that he was a hollow shell. Listening to him then felt like peering into his eyes that first time all over again.

"Hey," he said suddenly. "I'm sorry. I didn't mean to dump all that on you. Why don't we get another couple beers and something sweet? I have home-made ice cream in the fridge—churned it last week. I'll make you a beer float."

"A beer float? Wait, you *churned* ice cream? Like, by hand?" I couldn't keep my jaw from dropping.

"Oh, Gabe, tell me you don't eat the store-bought stuff and enjoy it?"

I tried to move my mouth, but words wouldn't come out. What did one even say to such a statement?

"Just trust me and come inside." He grinned, grabbed my hand, and pulled me into the kitchen.

Chapter 18

GABE

I watched as Devin stood on the box at the center of the pen, his head swiveling as the maelstrom of fluff raged around him. We'd had another busy morning, with more than twenty pups checking in for the day. If we kept up this rate, I'd have to take on more help and possibly add another fenced area, in addition to partitioning the existing one. The thought of my rapidly expanding business was at once exciting and terrifying.

Tam's hand on my arm brought my head around.

"You should twist his arm into working full-time. It would be a lot easier than having to break in someone new. Hiring is a pain."

I nodded. "I doubt he'll do it, but it's worth a try."

Her brow furrowed and she scrunched her nose. "What's going on in there? You're distracted today."

I tried to play it off, but a goofy grin betrayed any effort to hide the celebration going on inside my chest. It felt like fireworks from Fourth of July and New Year's all going off at the same time. I wanted to run and scream and laugh.

"Oh wow. You got laid, didn't you?"

I slapped her shoulder playfully. "No! I'm a gentleman, thank you very much."

She rolled her eyes. "How do you think *more* gentlemen are made? Well, not by *your* people, but in general."

"My people?" I laughed. "Who am I now, Moses?"

"You're gonna wish you were climbing a mountain if you don't start talking."

I waved my arms in the air and yelled, "Tamara, let my people go!"

She grabbed a pen from the desk and tossed it at my stomach.

"Hey. That's workplace abuse, and I'm now the leader of an ancient people. You should show a little respect."

She tossed herself into the desk chair and spun around once. "You're only delaying story time, you know that, right? I'm persistent—and I'm still waiting."

"Fine," I said, turning back to grab our only other chair and drag it to sit opposite her. "Ty invited me over for a dog park and dinner date."

Her eyes popped wide. "The same Tyler you were pining over all weekend? Mr. Miami?"

I nodded.

She leaned forward and rubbed her hands together, as if there was a campfire blazing between us. "Alright, go on. You *did* get laid, didn't you?"

"No! There was no laying with anyone last night. Like I said, we met at the dog park, hung out for an hour or so, then went to his place and had dinner. He grilled hamburgers."

She chuckled. "Burgers? Guess that rules out the guy knowing how to cook."

Both my brows shot up as another laugh escaped.

"What?" She leaned in.

"The guy's not what I thought. I mean, I thought he was nice and all, but he's not some dumb mechanic or a shallow pretty boy. He went to culinary school. His kitchen looks like something out of . . . I don't know. I've never seen anything like it. We had the best ice cream I've ever tasted—it was lavender flavored. He *made* it."

"What do you mean? Wait, *lavender*? Like the flower?"

I nodded. "It was like tasting that gentle, relaxing feeling you get from a lavender candle's aroma. It's so weird, but really good." Then I made a churning motion. "He made it from scratch, churned it in one of those old-fashioned wooden things with the big stick, like you see on TV when they're making butter, but different. He showed it to me. It looked really old."

"Wow. Okay, so he *can* cook. What else? Why do you think he's not some shallow gym bunny with perfect teeth?"

"Well, he kind of opened up last night, told me about his family and stuff they went through. The way he talked ... I don't know, Tam, he just seems deeper than I thought."

"Deeper? Is he reciting poetry alongside his ice cream churning?"

I tried not to giggle, but it slipped out. "There's just more to him than I thought. Every time I think I have him pegged, I learn something that surprises me. I mean, without any warning, he leaned over and kissed me full on the mouth, then just walked away to grill the meat. Didn't say a single word. I was so stunned I just stood there in his kitchen, staring after him."

"So you *did* get some!"

"Well—"

"I knew it. You had that glow that only comes when your cherry gets popped."

"Tam! Nobody even saw anybody's cherry ... and I'm pretty sure his cherry got chewed up and swallowed years ago."

"Eww. Okay, you are never allowed to make sexual references out of fruit again. You're terrible at it."

I chuckled. "You brought up cherries."

"Your cherry. I brought up *your* cherry because, if I am still correct, it's very much intact."

My head lowered. Her fingers lifted it up. "There's nothing wrong with waiting for someone special, Gabe. I admire you for it."

"Really?"

She gave me an odd smile, then said, "No. You need your brains fucked out. We'll all be a lot happier when that happens. Now, finish your story. Give me the short version. Dev looks like he's drowning out there."

I would never win with her. Why did I try?

"We talked for hours, even after dinner. Before I knew it, it was eleven o'clock. We'd been sitting on the couch with our fingers interlaced since nine. We both had early mornings, so I stood to go, but he grabbed me and pulled me into his chest. I swear, Tam, his body felt better than anything I've ever known. It was hard and warm—and soft—all at the same time. I don't even know how that's possible. He held me for the longest moment with his cheek pressed against the top of my head, then he gripped my shoulders and pulled me back to face him. The next thing I knew, our lips were locked and his tongue was gently grazing mine. I thought the world was going to spin off into the sky."

"Now we're getting somewhere. Then what?"

I shrugged. "We pulled apart and stared at each other for a minute. I found Audie and Dom snuggled up together in Dom's bed. It was pretty adorable. I leashed her, and he walked me to the door and kissed me good night. The end."

She blew out a sigh. "Alright, I'll admit it. That was pretty romantic for a burger date."

My giddy grin returned. "Yeah, it was."

"So, when are you seeing him again? Did you set another date?"

My grin widened. "Yep. Friday night, but we're meeting at the dog park again tonight. I think that's going to be our thing."

"Oh god. You're already planning *things*. This is bad."

"I know," I said, unable to contain another gleeful giggle.

Chapter 19

TYLER

Gabe and I met at the dog park every day after work for five straight days. Dom lost his mind each time we walked up to the double gate and found Audie waiting. Her tail was a blur of motion the moment my truck pulled into the lot.

Gabe grinned nearly as wide as Audie each time our eyes met. I didn't know what it was about that guy, but seeing him happy made the tightness in my chest release. Some crazy protective trigger tripped, and I just wanted to wrap him in my arms and make him feel safe. I didn't understand that—and it sure as hell made me uncomfortable—but I *think* I liked it. The dog park was starting to hold a different meaning each time I drove in that direction.

Friday afternoon, as I rolled beneath an ailing Mazda, my mind wandered to Gabe's grin. Deep-set dimples and floppy hair consumed my thoughts, and I swear the tea-tree scent of his hair gel drifted out of the Mazda's exhaust pipe.

"What are you doing down there?" Sam's gruff baritone startled me so badly I nearly banged my head. "You know we have a lift, right?"

"Yeah, I just needed a quick look at something." I wheeled myself back out to find Sam leaning against the car's side. "You don't have a tool in your hand. Just admiring your handiwork?"

"Somebody has to. My boss wouldn't know a compliment if it bit him."

"Ouch." He grabbed his shoulder like I'd punched him. "You wound me, good sir. Besides, I like a good nip in the right place."

I groaned as I shoved the wheely cart away and stood.

"Speaking of pleasure and pain, don't you have a big date tonight?"

"We're not dating."

He crossed his arms. "How many times have you seen Gabe this week?"

"The dog park doesn't count. It's a public space. It's not like we planned to meet there or anything," I said, a little too defensively.

"*Did* you plan to meet there?"

"You're such a fucker, you know that?"

He laughed. "So you *did* plan those trips. Miguel called it."

"What the hell? Are you two so bored with each other you've resorted to gambling on my love life?"

"Love life, is it? I thought you weren't even dating."

"I really hate you."

He unfurled his arms and wrapped me in a hug. "You love me, and you know it. I'm happy for you. Bring Gabe Sunday. Miguel wants to meet the guy brave enough to hang out with our baby boy."

I wanted to say something sharp, but the idea of introducing Gabe to the guys slapped me across the face. What's worse, the moment he suggested it, I really wanted to. Just thinking about introducing Gabe to my adopted family made something in my chest swell. Was that pride? Was I *proud* of Gabe? Did I want to show him off?

No, no, no. We're just friends. We're not dating. I will not date.

"Tell Mom I'll think about it," I said, instead of screaming like my internal voice begged me to do.

"Good. I'll tell Miguel to plan for four." He didn't give me a chance to argue, just spun and strode back into his office.

Chapter 20

TYLER

The restaurant Gabe picked out was closer to my condo than his apartment, so he parked in my lot and we took my truck together. I'm not sure why I was surprised he wanted to eat downtown, but he swore City House had the best handmade pasta in town, and I wasn't about to challenge a real Italian on his pasta recommendation. The restaurant itself wasn't much to look at. A couple rows of butcher-block-style tables and metal chairs stretched to the back. An open kitchen that also served bar seating consumed most of the other side. They'd left the ceiling open, and white bulbs dangled between silver A/C ducts that crisscrossed above. It was loud, a little rough, and smelled so good my stomach rumbled the moment we stepped inside.

The young woman who greeted us at the front door smiled broadly when she saw Gabe and immediately signed a *G* over her heart in welcome before wrapping him in a warm embrace. When she released him and stepped back, her eyes turned to me and widened slightly.

"And who is this? You've never brought anyone here before, young man."

Gabe blushed, so I stuck out my hand. "Hi. I'm Tyler."

She ignored my paw and wrapped me in the same tight hug. Her mouth neared my ear and she whispered, "Be good to him. He's the sweetest boy alive."

She pulled back and turned to Gabe as if the exchange had never happened. I was so taken aback that I had to remember to close my mouth. In a flash, we were seated in the center of the restaurant at a table for four. I thought it was a little odd when Gabe sat across from me. As much as I wanted to deny this was a date, I couldn't help feeling disappointed he'd sat so far away. Then I realized it made lipreading easier from that angle and felt stupid for feeling disappointed.

It was a lot of feelings for the beginning of a *non*-date, especially for me. I generally didn't have feelings.

"I love this place. I could just sit here and breathe in all the basil and garlic." He drew in a deep breath, held it, and closed his eyes, then blew it out and opened his eyes. "It reminds me of my mom's kitchen back home."

Gabe's smile was brilliant in the unshaded lights. I couldn't remember seeing someone look so genuinely happy as he did sitting there, staring across that table. Something in his innocent joy made all the clatter and chatter of the diners around us fade away.

"Is she a good cook?"

He nodded. "So good. She didn't go to cooking school like you though."

I chuckled. "Living in Italy is its own kind of culinary school. I'm jealous. I'd love to live there for a few years, really throw myself into the ingredients and culture."

There was an odd twinkle in his eyes as he stared for a moment without speaking. I grabbed my water glass and took a sip.

"Tell me about Sam and Miguel. You've mentioned them a few times. I know Sam's your boss, but the way you talk about them sounds more like family than friends."

I cocked my head. For a guy who couldn't hear, he sure didn't miss much.

"They are family. Sam and I moved here about the same time. He'd never lived anywhere with more people than cows, and I was just running from Pensacola, trying to figure out what I wanted to be when I grew up."

"Did you figure that out?"

I laughed. "Absolutely not. I'm still clueless."

He giggled, and my heart flared. That had to be the cutest sound in the world.

"Anyway, Sam opened his shop and asked me to work for him. I didn't have anything better to do, so I took the job. Been there ever since."

"Why didn't you work in a restaurant?"

"I don't know. I only went to culinary school because of my mom."

Now Gabe cocked his head.

"She loved to cook. It was kind of our thing together when I was little. She always told me I'd be a famous chef one day, made me promise to . . . Culinary school was me keeping that promise to her."

The server arrived with a bottle of wine Gabe had somehow secretly ordered without me seeing.

Colorful notes from the Chianti found their way to my nose. I took a sip and held it before swallowing.

"You like?" Gabe asked.

I nodded. "I'm more of a beer guy, but you know your grape juice."

He laughed so hard he nearly dropped his glass. "Grape juice?"

"Well, that's what it is, isn't it? Really old grape juice."

He shook his head. "You're terrible. I should've just taken you to a sports bar."

I winked. "I drove, so technically I brought you here. And, for the record, I love a good sports bar, especially if there's a good game on."

"Basketball, right?"

I nodded. "Only sport that matters. Don't let those idiot soccer players tell you otherwise."

"It's football. I've been in the States for eight years and I still can't call it soccer. And you're speaking blasphemy."

I watched over the rim of my glass as he laughed. That warm, tingly feeling snuck back into my chest.

"So." I set my glass down. "I know your family's back in Italy, but that's about it. You have a brother, right?"

He nodded. "Emilio. He's eighteen—no, nineteen—now."

"That's a big gap between you two."

He shrugged. "My mom calls him her 'oops.' I'm pretty sure having another kid wasn't in the plans after everything . . ." His eyes drifted and his fingers picked across a nick in the table. I sipped my wine and waited for him to look back up.

"As hard as it was for me, losing my hearing, I know it was terrible for them. They put their lives on hold to take me to a million doctors in the hope that one might know something all the others didn't. For a few years, we lived the rollercoaster of built-up hopes followed by soundless disappointment. My mom blamed herself. She tried to deny it, but I know she did. That was the worst."

"Gabe, I'm sorry." I had no idea what to say.

The server arrived with bread, mixed some olive oil, grated parmesan, and cracked pepper in a small dish, then took our orders. The bread had cheese packed into the center that oozed when we pulled it apart. If Gabe could've heard the moan I let out when I took that first bite, he might've run for the door. It was heaven on a plate.

"Anyway, Emilio's the best. Him coming along worked for us like your stepmom did for you and your dad. He couldn't give me back my hearing, but he healed our hearts."

"You miss him, don't you?"

"Oh yeah. So much. He was eleven when I left, and I've only been back to Italy twice in all those years. He's grown so much I barely recognized him last time."

"He should come visit you here. I bet he'd love the academy."

Gabe lit up again. "We used to exercise Dad's dogs together, do some basic training too. He's a natural. Guess growing up around it helps."

We reached for the bread at the same time and played tug-of-war until it ripped apart. Gabe held up his much larger chunk like it was an Olympic medal. Mine was little more than a piece of crust between my fingers. I pooched out my lip.

"Aw, poor Ty. Here, let me make it all better." He tore his piece and handed me half, then sopped up the last of the olive oil mixture. When I looked aghast at the empty dish, he shrugged and said, "I gave you bread out of pity. You'll have to get your own oil."

I feigned offense. "You little rat. I see how you are now."

He giggled again, and I thought my heart might burst.

The server arrived with our meals, refilled our wine, and vanished again. By the time I'd eaten half my bowl of pasta, I felt like my stomach might burst. Gabe, on the other hand, had nearly cleaned his plate and looked like he could eat the rest of mine.

"How?" I said with wide eyes.

He noticed my hand covering my belly and chuckled. "What can I say? I'm a growing boy."

He was thin, not to an unhealthy extent, but he didn't have the layers of beef I did. Where he put all that food was a mystery. How he kept from weighing eight hundred pounds was another.

When a plate of towering tiramisu arrived, I pushed my chair back and stood.

"You okay? This is really amazing stuff."

I grinned. "I need to go make room before I eat another bite. Be right back."

His giggle serenaded me all the way to the restroom.

Once firmly ensconced on the throne, I grabbed my phone. There was one text message waiting.

Sam: So, how's it going? Miguel wants to know if you've invited him for Sunday yet.

ME: CAN WE FINISH THIS DATE FIRST, PLEASE? GOD, YOU TWO ARE SUCH AN OLD MARRIED COUPLE.

SAM: WE TAKE THAT AS HIGH PRAISE, ESPECIALLY COMING FROM A SLUT LIKE YOU.

ME: SLUT? I'M OFFENDED. IN FACT . . . WELL . . . I RESEMBLE THAT REMARK.

SAM: AND THERE IT IS. PROSECUTION RESTS.

ME: ISN'T PUTTING PEOPLE AWAY MOM'S JOB?

SAM: HE'S GOING TO PUT YOU AWAY IF YOU DON'T BRING PUDDIN' OVER ON SUNDAY. I KNOW YOU'RE PROBABLY ON THE TOILET, OTHERWISE YOU WOULDN'T BE TEX-

TING. GET YOUR SHIT OVER WITH AND GO
ASK HIM BEFORE MIGUEL SENDS ME OUT TO
FIND YOU.

ME: HE WOULDN'T.

SAM: HE WOULD.

ME: UGH. YOU'RE RIGHT. HE WOULD. BYE,
DAD.

I laid my head back against the tiled wall and laughed. I really did have the best friends.

When I returned to the table, the dessert stood untouched.

"You didn't have to wait for me."

"Of course I did. I wanted to see you take your first bite." That childlike twinkle was back in Gabe's eyes.

"It's that good?"

He shrugged, scooped up a bite with a spoon, and reached it across the table toward my mouth. I tried not to focus on the couple at the table beside us as they watched the exchange, but they were staring.

"Sweet mother of pearl," I said through a full mouth of Italian ecstasy.

Gabe giggled again. "I have no idea what you said, but I'm guessing it's good."

I nodded and chewed.

He grabbed another spoon and attacked.

Damn, that boy could eat.

By the time we downed the last of our wine, and Gabe scraped the last of the chocolate from the plate, the sky was darkening outside. As we exited the restaurant onto Fourth Avenue, Gabe let out a contented sigh.

"Feels good to be stuffed," I said.

He nodded and rubbed his stomach. "I'm so full. Want to walk it off before we head back?"

The air was crisp, and Gabe's face held the same wide-eyed longing I often saw in Dom when he wanted another walk, so I nodded. "Absolutely."

It took ten minutes of leisurely strolling to cross Jefferson Street and step onto the grass of the Bi-centennial Mall, a sprawling park that stretched lengthwise toward the State Capital, similar to the Mall in Washington, DC, just on a smaller scale. We were passing the first of several fountains when I realized, somewhere along our route, our hands had clasped. Neither of us had said any-thing, and I didn't remember consciously decid-ing to do it. Oddly, when I realized our fingers were entangled, I didn't pull away. It felt nice.

I'd never held a guy's hand in public. Nashville had come a long way over the years, but it was still the buckle of the Bible Belt. Public displays of affection by two men or two women wouldn't necessarily get an egg tossed your way, but they weren't exactly popular either.

In that moment, as I considered the warmth of Gabe's palm and the perpetual grin on his face, I realized I didn't care what the world thought. If I wanted to hold Gabe's hand as we enjoyed an evening in the park, so be it. Screw everybody else and their ogling eyes.

Just then I caught an older man and woman watching us from a nearby park bench. The path led us right past them. There was no way around. A wave of disquiet washed over me as we neared, but Gabe chose that moment to ex-press his contentment through a firm squeeze, eliminating any chance I could let go and pretend we hadn't been holding hands.

As we passed the elderly couple, bony fingers gripped my wrist and halted our progress. I steeled myself for the sermon to come. Gabe simply turned so he could see what caused me to stop walking.

"Young man," the woman said. "You two make the most beautiful pair. It warms my old heart to see boys like you two in love."

I was sure my eyes bugged out. I croaked out a "thank you," and the woman freed my arm. My eyes darted from her husband to Gabe, then back to her. I couldn't speak. She'd assumed . . . she'd thought . . . Then I looked down at our hands, still snug in their embrace, and I felt Gabe's shoulder press against mine. I couldn't decide if I wanted to wrap my arm around him or run in the other direction toward my truck. Before panic could seize my throat more than it already had, I nodded to the couple and pulled Gabe along the path, marching double-time away from that bench and its occupants.

We'd made it twenty or so paces when Gabe's voice shattered my frantic thoughts.

"What was that all about? Did she want something?"

We stopped and faced each other. For the first time in a while, our hands parted.

"She . . . uh . . . she just . . ."

His brow furrowed. "Are you okay?"

"Yeah, I'm good. She just wanted to know what time it was, that's all."

He eyed me a second, then nodded and turned to continue walking. We cut across the center path, then turned back toward the restaurant. I couldn't stop the woman's voice from playing again and again in my head. Why had she gotten to me? What was it about an old lady being sweet that had me so rattled?

Then my fingers rubbed together, and I realized my palm was empty.

It felt empty.

I reached over and took Gabe's palm in mine. He glanced up and the brightest smile possible bloomed on his face. With his other hand, he reached across his body and rubbed my arm and leaned into me. It was the most affectionate, intimate thing I'd felt from a guy in . . . ever.

We didn't speak again on that walk.

I couldn't speak again. I didn't know what to say.

When we got in the truck, Gabe fastened his seat belt, then turned and said, "This was the best date I think I've ever had. Thank you."

The lump I thought I'd rid myself of back in the park slammed into my throat so hard I thought it must've done permanent damage. I tried to say something, even though I had no idea what would come out if my mouth actually opened, so I did the only thing that came to mind: I reached across the truck, gripped Gabe's face in both hands, and pulled him in to my lips.

Chapter 21

GABE

When Ty pulled me in for a kiss, my whole world stopped. I thought my heart would never beat again. His lips tasted of Chianti and olive oil, and held passion and tenderness I didn't know could coexist in one touch. I don't know how long we remained frozen like that, but my ribs started to ache from the center console, and I had to pull back. I'd never forgive Ford for putting that darn thing in between our seats.

When our lips parted, he looked away, then back. "Was that okay? I didn't think . . . I wasn't thinking."

I ignored my wounded side and leaned over and silenced his questions. This time tenderness turned to passion, which fanned a hunger I'd never felt. Our tongues met and teased and danced. His hands flew to the back of my head and fingers buried themselves in my hair. Only when his elbow hit the horn did we both jump and pull back, laughing like a pair of schoolboys caught smoking behind the gym.

"Let's go home," he said, turning the key.

Before we'd pulled out of the parking lot, he'd reached over and pulled my hand onto the center console. When he entwined our fingers again, I forgave Ford and allowed my arm to relax against the cushion.

Ty's thumb rubbed back and forth the whole drive.

When he shut off the truck, safely parked back at his condo, he turned and asked, "Want to come inside for a bit?"

I nodded, and nearly choked when he raised my hand to his lips.

Domino greeted us at the door. As much as I craved more kisses from Ty, I did the only thing any self-respecting dog lover could do in that situation: I dropped onto the floor and rolled around with Dom until he licked me wet. By the time he let me sit up, Ty had tossed off his shoes and was grinning from ear to ear as he watched us play.

"He really likes you."

I wiped slobber off my face as Dom, responding to Tyler's voice, abandoned me for his human.

"What? Did you say something?"

Ty ruffled Dom's hair. "He really likes you."

"Most dogs do. People are a different challenge."

Ty pushed Dom aside, closed the gap between us, and pulled me to my feet. I'd barely gained my balance before his arms were wrapped around me.

"You do pretty well with people too. This one likes you."

The room suddenly turned warm.

Ty kissed me again, and I forgot about dogs and temperatures. I wrapped my arms around him and, holy shit, his body was insane. I pushed us apart and put my hands on his chest, then felt through his shirt at his abs. It was like rubbing stones.

"Jesus, you're hard as a rock."

His grin turned lecherous, and he grabbed my wrist and pushed my hand against his jeans. "You have no idea."

My eyes popped wide. "Fuck. I do now."

I was about to say something else—I had no idea what—when his lips assaulted mine again. He reached around and lifted me off my feet, moving us both onto the couch where his body smothered me into the cushions.

There was no more thinking. My hands roamed up his back, then down to grip his butt. As we kissed, I gripped his shirt and pulled it up so my hands could feel his skin unhindered. He was smooth, and the muscles of his back rippled with every motion. I groaned as he ground his cock into me.

He sat upright and slowly pulled his shirt over his head, revealing the body I'd seen in my dreams since the first days I knew I was gay. I reached up and touched his chest again. His hand joined mine and pressed my flesh into his. Then he raised my palm to his lips and kissed it. Then he kissed my wrist. Then an inch further. Then again, and again, until he'd traversed my arm and was trailing his teeth across my shoulder. I arched my back and waves rolled through me. I'd never felt—

"I've never—"

"What?" Ty sat up. "I didn't hear you. What did you say?"

My eyes darted from his face to his arms, then his chest. I didn't know where to look anymore.

"I . . . uh . . . I've never been . . . you know . . . with a guy."

Tyler gaped.

An eternity passed.

"You . . . what? Really? Never?"

I shook my head, suddenly more self-conscious than I'd been in recent memory. All pent-up sexual tension fled, and my raging hard-on turned into an innie faster than you can say "belly button."

Ty sat up on his knees, straddling me on the couch.

God, he was beautiful.

I couldn't tell what the look in his eyes meant. Was he disappointed? Surely he'd been with guys before. Probably a bunch of them. He was hot enough to have anyone he wanted. Now that he knew I'd never gone past first base, he'd probably lose all interest.

I squirmed out from under him and huddled on the far side of the couch with my legs pulled to my chest.

He smiled. It looked like pity or . . . something.

Then he closed the gap between us and took my face in his hands like he'd done in the truck. My heart threatened to beat out of my chest again. I could barely breathe.

"Gabe, I want you so bad it hurts, but not like this, not your first time. That should be special, something you remember forever."

I couldn't pull myself from his gaze.

"Was your first time special?"

"No. Not even close." He laughed, and his hands dropped away. "I was fifteen. A guy on the wrestling team followed me to my car after a basketball game. He was probably the hottest guy in school, and nobody knew he was gay. I found out that night."

"Were you friends?"

He shook his head. "Hadn't really ever talked. I wasn't walking around waving a rainbow flag or anything, but I hadn't kept it a secret that I liked boys—at least, I thought I did. I was fifteen. What did I know?"

My arms were pinned so I gave him an eye shrug. "Sound like you knew pretty well, after all."

"Guess so." He chuckled. "Are you okay if we stop here?"

He must've seen the hurt cross my face. "Hey," he said, cupping my cheek with his palm again. "I'm not going anywhere. This is a big deal, and I want it to be right for you. That's all."

"Promise?"

"Pinky swear." His teeth nearly blinded me as he held up a hooked little finger.

I smacked his bare chest and laughed. "You're such an ass."

"Funny, that's what Sam says all the time."

For once, I knew how Audie felt when I finally gave in and grabbed her favorite ball for a park trip. I couldn't stop grinning, and felt like I wanted to run laps around my car. On the way home, I rolled down the windows and blasted the radio. It could've been spewing static throughout the neighborhood for all I could hear, but it felt like the right thing to do when my mood was stretching itself toward the starry sky. I'd never known it was even possible to feel this good.

Ty really liked me.

Me. The deaf kid from Italy who nearly ran home to his mom after a few months in the US.

I shouted out the window, drawing confused glances from drivers stopped at the same red light. I didn't care. Let them stare. Tyler Hyatt, Nashville's hottest mechanic, liked me. That's all that mattered.

I didn't care that we'd stopped at second base. Hell, I'd never rounded first before. I ran my fingers over my lips, begging them to tingle like they had when he'd kissed me, when his tongue teased every curve and crease. I could still feel his chest and arms. His body towered before me, a living statue of marble or, more likely in Tennessee, quartz, but that sounded weird. Who made a Greek god statue out of quartz? He'd be all sparkly and . . . I giggled at the thought of him having sparkly balls, like little disco balls hanging below his cock.

And then I was thinking about his cock.

Damn. I hadn't even seen it, but when he pressed my hand against it so I could feel it through his jeans, I thought I might die right there.

As a wise Klingon in *Star Trek* once said, "It would've been a good death."

The clock on my dash flipped eleven o'clock, so I turned the stereo off. It had been tuned to FM 90.3, which I thought was Nashville's public channel, maybe the classical music station. I wasn't sure. The thought of blaring Wagner through the streets of downtown made me chuckle. Then again, after the night I'd just had with Ty, everything made me chuckle.

I was a serial chuckler. A repeat giggler. A giggle monster.

Yeah, giggle monster—that fit.

The silly nickname made me giggle louder.

God, it had been the best day ever.

Chapter 22

TYLER

At six o'clock, Dom decided Daddy had slept long enough.

"Buddy, please. Daddy doesn't have to work today and needs to sleep. Go watch cartoons or something."

Undeterred, he edged forward and planted his front paws on my chest. When I still didn't rise, his tongue dove into my ear like a diver searching for wreckage. I bolted upright.

"Fine. I'm up. Jesus," I said, failing miserably to reach the slobber now embedded near my bleary brain.

An hour later, Dom and Daddy had both eaten. Daddy lay stretched on the couch, nursing his third cup of coffee, while his ever-present shadow pawed at his arm.

Jab. Jab, jab.

"What now?"

Jab, jab.

I made the slightest motion to rise, and he bolted toward the door. By the time I stood and turned, he was sitting with the leash in his mouth.

Smart beast.

I couldn't suppress a smile—and a hint of pride. *That's my boy.*

"It's a quarter past seven. I'm not sure anybody'll be at the park, but we can go check it out."

Dom's tail blurred, and he began to whimper excitedly.

A couple hours later, we sat on the patio of a local café. Dom was worn out from the park and slept peacefully at my feet while I sipped more coffee and munched on a more proper breakfast than the power bar I'd eaten earlier.

It was another breathtaking fall day in Nashville. The air was cool but comfortable, and the sun shone brilliantly above, with only a few patchy clouds drifting lazily by.

"I feel you, clouds," I said, as I absently gazed upward.

My phone buzzed.

I was surprised to find a text from Marcus, a trainer at my gym I'd hooked up with a number of times after long nights at Shadow Box. We usually just ran into each other. He rarely texted.

DEVILTATMARCUS: YO.

ME: YO, YOURSELF.

DEVILTATMARCUS: DOING THE BOX TONIGHT? I COULD USE SOME GREASE UNDER MY NAILS . . . OR WHEREVER YOU WANT TO PUT IT.

I grinned as my silky shorts tickled my suddenly throbbing head. Marcus was a lot of fun, and had an ass you could break a tooth on—at least, I enjoyed testing that theory.

But another text came through before I could respond.

DEAF DIMPLES: MORNING, HANDSOME.

A completely different warmth flooded through me when I saw Gabe's words. I ignored Marcus and typed a reply to Gabe.

ME: GOOD MORNING, MISTER.

DEAF DIMPLES: I COULDN'T SLEEP LAST NIGHT. THANKS A LOT FOR THAT.

ME: WHAT DID I DO?

DEAF DIMPLES: YOU MADE ME THINK ABOUT YOU ALL NIGHT. I COULDN'T GET YOUR LIPS OUT OF MY MIND.

ME: JUST MY LIPS?

DEAF DIMPLES: WELL, I MIGHT'VE THOUGHT ABOUT YOUR CHEST ONCE. AND MAYBE YOUR ARMS A COUPLE TIMES.

ME: USE ME FOR MY BODY. I SEE HOW YOU ARE.

DEAF DIMPLES: LOL YEAH, THAT'S ME. USE 'EM AND TOSS 'EM.

ME: I KNEW THERE WAS A RED FLAG I WAS MISSING!

Marcus chimed in.

DEVIL TAT MARCUS: SO, YOU IN?

Then Gabe texted.

DEAF DIMPLES: WANT TO CONTINUE WHERE WE LEFT OFF TONIGHT? IF YOU'RE BRAVE ENOUGH, I BELIEVE IT'S MY TURN TO COOK. YOU CAN BRING DOM, MAKE IT A DOUBLE DATE.

I flipped to the screen showing all my texts stacked together. Gabe's was on top, followed by the preview of Marcus's, then several others from earlier in the week. The dots didn't bounce on either of their texts. They were each waiting for me.

If I went to the club, it would be a wild night followed by even wilder sex. Shadow Box never let me down, and Marcus was a sure bet.

On the other hand, Gabe was . . . well, I didn't know what Gabe was. I barely knew what he made me feel. It was like drinking a beer at the end of a long day in the hot garage, both refreshing and comforting. I was sure he'd giggle at me comparing him to an alcoholic beverage, and something in the memory of that sound made me grin.

If I blew Marcus off, there'd always be another time. I wasn't going anywhere, and there was definitely no danger of him settling down or dating.

And there was that word again.

Dating.

If I went to Gabe's for dinner, a second evening in a row, a third in less than a week, did that mean we were dating? Between the dinners, we'd planned park visits every night. I tried to tell myself those were for Dom—and they sort of were—but I knew better. I'd looked forward to seeing him as I'd left work each afternoon. There was something reassuring in his persistent presence in my evenings I hadn't known before. I hadn't really thought about it much, and the exercise made my stomach churn uncomfortably.

My phone buzzed again. It was Marcus.

DEVILTATMARCUS: YOU THERE?

I opened the chain from Gabe, then switched to Marcus, then back. My stomach lurched and my head started pounding. Why was this such a hard choice? Saturdays were party nights. At least, they always had been.

I stopped thinking and let my fingers move on their own.

ME: I CAN'T TONIGHT. ANOTHER NIGHT?

Chapter 23

GABE

I tossed my phone on the couch and let Audie hop up beside me for a nuzzle. Ever vigilant, she sensed my mood and knew I needed her presence.

"Come here, *dolcezza*. Papa needs you to keep him calm."

Her whole rear end wagged at my pet name for the sweetest girl in the world.

"I can't believe it either. Ty and Dom are coming here for dinner!"

When I opened the door and saw Ty standing there, with Domino sitting patiently by his side, my heart leapt into my throat. He wore a form-fitting

T-shirt the color of a ripe avocado that made his emerald eyes richer and more vibrant. It did nice things for his chest and arms too.

Audie, far less shy than her papa, shot past me and bowled into Domino. Before either of the humans could react, Audie had greeted Dom and dragged him back inside so he could inspect the new space he was entering.

When I glanced back toward Ty, his eyes were dancing. "They really love each other."

I grinned and nodded. "Guess they do. Come on in."

I was going to wait politely as Ty entered, but he had no such notion of propriety, taking one long stride forward and wrapping his arms around my waist. He wasn't tentative or shy. He stepped up and took me like I was his, lifting me off the ground and into his body, then smothering my mouth with his lips.

This time I tasted cherry, or maybe strawberry. I giggled at him upping his lip flavor game.

"What are you giggling at now?" I read him say. His eyes were doing that sparkly jazz dance again.

"You taste good. Kinda fruity." I giggled again.

"I'll show you fruity, bucko." He dug his fingers into my sides and began tickling the shit out of me. I must've yelled or laughed really loud because Audie came charging and knocked Ty off balance, freeing me from his grip. By the time I realized what had happened, my pooch was standing with all fours spread and her ears at attention in a protective posture between us.

"Easy, girl. I was just tickling your daddy," Ty said, holding up a palm.

I grinned. "You really shouldn't offer your hand to an angry dog. They might take you up on the invitation."

Domino glanced between Audie and Ty, as if considering whose side to pick.

I laughed, and Audie relaxed her stance. Dom trotted over and nudged my hand with his nose, completely ignoring his human lying on the ground a pace away.

"Really? You little traitor."

My next giggle earned a scowl from my fallen date.

With the dogs settled and resting beside each other in the den, Ty and I sat at my pub table and chatted over our chicken and veggies.

When the plates were empty, he insisted on helping me carry everything into the kitchen. He even dried dishes while I washed. Our shoulders bumped together as I handed him plates and glasses. He made some smart-ass remark about me prewashing my dishes before putting them into the dishwasher, so I squirted him with the sprayer. That started a full-blown water war right there in my kitchen.

When our laughter calmed, I grabbed a kitchen towel and turned to dab Ty's shirt dry. He ripped the towel out of my hand and tossed it across the apartment, then gripped the bottom of his shirt and pulled it over his head. Before I could blink, it rested on top of the towel near the dog bed.

"Ty—"

He didn't let me speak, just grabbed my wrists, pulled them up over my head and gripped them in one hand, then pulled my shirt up and over my head with the other. I'd barely taken two breaths before we were both standing in my kitchen half-naked.

I suddenly felt unbearably skinny.

"I love how much smaller you are than me. Your body is so sexy," he said, as he read my mind and ran his fingers over my chest for the first time. "I've been thinking about this all day."

"Really?" My eyes were saucers. "What . . . what were you thinking?"

The only answer I got was his teeth brushing against my neck, and his hands gripping my butt cheeks, kneading them like he was prepping sour-dough to rise.

I'd never had my dough kneaded before.

Bread was fucking hot.

I raised my hands to grip his back, but he grabbed my wrists again and pulled them behind me.

"No, no. Tonight is all about you."

I cocked my head like Audie had done earlier.

"Let me show you how much I like you, please. Just let me enjoy you."

What the fuck was I supposed to say to that?

I let out a whimper as his finger trailed my nipple, then nodded like the scared rabbit I was.

That's all the permission he needed.

Gentler than I could've imagined, Ty lifted and cradled me in his arms, then carried me into the den, where he laid me on the couch. Our lips parted only long enough to breathe, and I suddenly knew what a Disney princess felt as she was magically transported to another place and time.

Ty pulled my arms above my head again. "Leave those there, okay?"

I nodded again, unable to speak.

His lips pressed into mine, then traveled to my chin, then my neck and collarbone. Each kiss brought him lower, from nipples to abs. His fingers trailed along my sides, sending chills across my skin. He said something into my stomach, I'll never know what, but the rumbling vibration of his voice and echo of his breath—

"God, Ty."

He gripped the top of my shorts in his teeth.

My cock pressed against his chin. I could feel it pulsing, twitching, begging to be freed and touched.

Ever so slowly, Ty lifted my butt and moved his whole body toward my feet, dragging my shorts off in a motion I'd only seen in porn. I thought I might explode right there.

I dared a glance down and saw him smile as he eyed my tighty whities, then realized he wasn't looking at the fabric, but the fruit of *my* loom. I was harder than I could ever remember. Staring down, a jolt of pride snuck into my chest, and a giggle slipped out.

Ty's eyes shot up to mine. They were so pure, so sweet. They laughed with me . . . until they lowered to my cock and fire bloomed where emeralds sparkled before.

He put his mouth over the outline of my cock in my undies, barely touching the cloth, teasing my tender senses below. Every time he brushed against it, my whole body jerked. A moment later, he rose to his knees and took the top of my underwear in his teeth like he had with my shorts. Just as slowly as before, he dragged them downward. When I was finally freed, he rubbed his cheek against my shaft and kissed its base. Once, twice, then he ran his tongue over my balls and up the throbbing blue vein until his lips hovered above my tip. The warmth of his breath tickled and taunted. My body begged for him to take me whole.

And he heard it.

His mouth opened and the whole of my cock vanished down his throat. I could feel the warmth inside him, coating my skin, lapping up my desire. I was inside Tyler. He was breathing me, sucking me . . .

"Oh shit!"

He was swallowing me.

I tried to pull away, to pull out, but his hands held me in place. I spasmed over and over, and he swallowed every shot. Long after my last load, he kept me inside his mouth, held me there, caressed me with his tongue.

I couldn't suppress a shiver as I lay back, my energy spent.

The warmth of his mouth finally vanished, and he moved onto the couch, rolling me onto my side so he could hold me from behind. I pressed myself into his body, willing myself to melt into him as his muscular arms enveloped my whole being.

When the dogs came to investigate, we didn't move. Tyler didn't budge.

I lost track of how long we laid there, tangled together on my couch.

I'd never felt so safe.

Audie's tongue tickling my hand woke me up. Two bleary-eyed boys stumbled outside to let their pups pee.

"Shit, it's past midnight. I should probably go, let you get some rest." Dom finished marking every bush he could find and Ty turned toward me.

I pressed my hand to his chest. "You could stay. There's a great little breakfast place around the corner. Sundays are kind of their thing."

He stared a moment, then his lips curled upward. "On one condition."

My brows rose. "I didn't realize this was a negotiation."

"Always," he chuckled. "After breakfast, you come with me to Sam and Miguel's place. They cook out every Sunday, and they've been giving me shit about bringing you this week."

My mouth dropped open. "They know about me? I mean, they know who I am?"

Ty froze, like he'd just realized something, then nodded.

His friends knew about me.

My face flushed with heat, and whatever wild animal that lived in my chest chose that moment to wake and bounce off my ribs. I wanted to jump and run and shout and scream.

"Your smile is so big," Ty said.

I giggled.

He leaned down and kissed me. "Let's go inside. You're going to need your rest before meeting Sam and Miguel. Trust me on that."

Chapter 24

TYLER

Dom had my internal clock so tightly wound that I woke up at precisely six o'clock. Gabe's body was nuzzled against mine. Every part of his body that could touch my skin was pressed into me. His hair tickled my nose. I breathed in his scent, and my eyes closed as I felt him adjust and settle without waking.

Not too long ago, I'd woken up next to someone in a bed I didn't own, in a city that didn't claim me. I thought it had been fun. Hell, it *had* been fun—but the emptiness in my chest that begged to be filled refused whatever that man had offered.

Who was I kidding?

All he'd offered was dick and ass. That's all they ever offered.

Did they even know there was more out there, more worth having? For the first time in my nearly thirty years, I thought I saw hints of hues where before there had only been shades of gray.

We'd both been so high, we wouldn't have known a real emotion if ... no, there was no way either of us would've known anything real; not that night, not *any* night.

Laying there with Gabe, holding him in my arms, feeling his chest swell with every breath, something stirred in me that I didn't understand. I scooted so he rested on his back, so I could watch him sleep. His eyes darted beneath his lids, and a smile creased his lips. I wondered what filled his dreams with joy.

I wondered if I might be somewhere in his sleeping mind.

I brushed his hair back from his forehead, curled a lock behind his ear. I wanted to reach inside and find what had failed, to return whatever he'd lost. His deafness hadn't divided us, but it did make us different in ways we could never erase. Something in that realization hurt. I felt it. Deep within my chest, I ached for his loss, for the cruel gulf between us.

Like I had every other moment we'd shared, I consciously dismissed his impairment and trailed my fingers across his cheek, careful not to wake him. His skin was so perfect; unblemished. His olive complexion contrasted against the copper tones of my own.

My gaze wandered down his slim neck to his arms and stomach. A trail of wispy hair begged to be touched, to be teased and licked. His taut runner's build was so different from my muscled frame, so different from those I'd sought on my wild weekends away; and yet, I couldn't pull my eyes away. I didn't want to—

"Morning."

I nearly jumped out of the bed. The sheet kept me from falling backward.

"How long have you been awake?"

He grinned. "Long enough to watch you taking a visual tour of my body."

I pulled him into me and kissed his neck. "I really like your body."

He blushed and tried to look away. I reached up and held his eyes to mine. "You don't ever have to be embarrassed with me, not ever. I really like you, Gabe. More than ... well, a lot."

Shit, where had that come from?

"I really like you too, Ty."

He craned his head upward and kissed me.

"What time is it?" he asked when we came up for air.

"From the way Dom's pacing at the foot of the bed, I'd say around six thirty. He's annoyingly punctual in the mornings."

Gabe chuckled. "Let's take them out. If it's not too early for you, we can get breakfast before the church crowd mobs the place."

Gabe had been right about breakfast. The place was quirky as hell.

The servers wore white diner uniforms trimmed in red and blue, which wouldn't have been unusual if each hadn't also worn a hat of a different movie genre. Our waiter was the western dude, sporting a cowboy hat and boots with spurs that jingled as he approached our table.

The menu played a similar game, taking traditional breakfast items, giving them some odd twist, then rebranded them with an offbeat name that included a celebrity. I had the Eggs Benedict Cumberbatch. Instead of ham, this dish featured a layer of crab. I'm not sure what they were trying to say about poor Mr. C. Gabe giggled as he ordered the Jane Fondue. Diners around us craned their necks

and pointed when his meal was present-
ed. It consisted of a plate of cube-shaped,
bite-sized waffles, French toast, pancakes, and
sausages decoratively arranged around two dip-
ping bowls. They even provided a long fork for
spearing and dunking. A quick glance at the
menu told me that meal was designed to feed
two people. Gabe hadn't noticed that bit of fine
print—or was undeterred by it, as he wolfed
down every last bite.

We had a few hours before the boys expected
us, so we went back to Gabe's apartment and
walked the dogs. Once back inside, Gabe turned
to me and wrinkled his nose.

"What?"

He waved a finger up and down my shirt. It
was so badly wrinkled, the guys would think I'd
slept in it, and there was a spot where I'd dribbled
something at dinner or been licked by a dog with
a dirty tongue.

"Take that off. I'll run it through on quick
wash. We'll have just enough time."

"You just want me to sit around your apartment without my shirt, don't you?"

He giggled. "Maybe. Now, strip."

I dropped my pants and stood there, balls flopping freely. Underwear was for wimps.

He gaped, then stepped forward, gripped my shirt, and pulled it upward. I raised my arms to let him strip me naked.

By the time the shirt was free, his lips were pressed to mine and I was hard again.

"You stay," he said, giving me Audie's hand signal for *stay*. I glanced behind me and both dogs sat watching the training session with interest. Gabe's giggle followed as he snatched my shirt and shorts and strode through the kitchen into the laundry room. When he returned, he stopped a few paces away and roamed my body with his eyes.

"You really are like a living magazine cover."

"Stop." I felt an unfamiliar rush of heat travel into my cheeks.

"Oh my god, you're blushing. Tyler Hyatt just blushed. Let me go mark the calendar."

The heat flared. "Ha ha. I'm standing here naked. What did you expect?"

His humor morphed into hunger. "I expect you to find a creative way to spend the next hour while your clothes wash."

I grinned, then crossed my arms. "Okay. I see how you are. Take your shirt off."

"Right here?" He glanced around, his eyes eventually landing on the dogs. "The kids will see."

I shrugged. "Kids gotta learn sometime. Might do them good. Now: Shirt. Off." I made the same motion he'd given me a moment earlier.

This time he blushed.

It was freakin' adorable.

I closed the gap between us and traced a finger along scratches on his hands and arms.

"Battle wounds from the academy."

I raised his wrist and kissed the back of his hand once, then again. The smile that bloomed on his face swelled my chest.

I glanced down.

"You want to take those off, or you want me to do it?"

His thumb was hooked in his waistband.

"Uh, I can . . . no, you do it."

I kissed him while my hands slipped inside his shorts, one on each hip, then held them there. His skin felt warm beneath my touch. I gripped him and pulled him into me so I could feel him stiffen. I'd already leaked a bead of slickness, and the friction of his shorts against my skin quickly turned into slippery ecstasy. He grabbed my face. Gentle kisses became urgent passion. My hands slid down so his shorts would fall away, and we stood in his den, naked, and kissed until neither of us could take it anymore.

"I want you inside me," Gabe said through panted breaths.

I pulled back, my eyes wide.

"Really? Are you sure? I mean—"

"Ty, you are special. This is special. Please." His eyes were steady, and there was no doubt in his voice.

I considered this beautiful, innocent man standing naked before me. He was so pure, such a *good* guy, and here he was, offering himself to me. I would be his first. I'd never been anyone's first. I'd had more sex than I could remember, but this was . . . intimidating? No, overwhelming. It felt like taking something I really enjoyed and raising it to a whole other level. Was this the next step in . . . ? Were we? My head spun.

Gabe's fingers circled my nipples, teasing them to life and sending flares of ice and fire down my spine.

I couldn't think anymore, couldn't consider or debate or doubt.

All I could see was Gabe, how badly I wanted him, to feel him against me, to feel him *inside* me.

Where the hell—?

He wrapped his arms around my nakedness and consumed my mouth with his tongue and lips. He clawed at my back, sending streaks of fire where his fingernails grazed.

"What if you—"

My brows shot upward as his eyes grinned with ravenous desire.

Without parting, we kicked off our shorts now clinging to our feet, then shuffled together into his bedroom, ignoring the curious dogs who'd glared throughout the entire undressing. When we reached the bed, Gabe sat and held his palms against my chest to keep me standing. He stared at my cock, now twitching at his eye level, then leaned forward and ran his tongue over its head, then along the fold where my foreskin had stretched when I'd hardened. I was so sensitive. My whole body shivered.

"You're uncut." He traced my taut skin with a finger.

"Uh–huh." He hadn't looked up, but I was sure he felt my grunt somehow. His eyes drifted up to meet mine. "I like that. More to play with."

I ran my fingers into his hair. It was so full and messy, flopping and curing in every direction. He couldn't have been any cuter than he was in that moment.

All thought—or whatever—vanished as his eyes turned downward and he took my head in his mouth. His tongue slid over my already slick tip, and I spasmed into his touch. With one hand, he gripped my based and balls and gently pulled downward, stretching my skin to its fullest length, then sank further down my shaft. I could feel his throat as his lips tickled my pubes. I spasmed again, and he gagged, pulling back a moment to catch his breath.

When he glanced up, embarrassment in his eyes, I grinned. "I'm a big boy."

"That's for sure." His eyes glittered, then fell as he took me in his mouth again.

When my legs began to buckle, I shuffled around and lay on my back on his bed. He managed to make the turn without taking me out of his mouth.

For a rookie, he sure is agile.

His hand found its way between my legs, then a finger wedged its way into my cheeks. He regained his rookie status as he tried to spear my hole with his un-lubed middle finger.

"Ow," I said, gently gripping his wrist.

He froze, his eyes wide. "I'm sorry. Did I do something—"

I smiled. "Lube up your finger first. I wasn't planning any of this, but I think I'm okay back there."

It took a split second for recognition to dawn, but the mix of excitement and disgust that crossed his features was too much. I spit out a laugh.

He slapped my chest playfully as he reached across my body to the nightstand and retrieved a small bottle and squirted clear liquid into his palm. Seconds later, his finger returned and slid easily inside me. My eyes were closed, and I didn't see him take me in his mouth again. His finger slid past the knuckle and his throat opened to take the whole of my cock. I arched my back and groaned, willing myself deeper into him, him into me. He pulled his finger back, then slid it deeper. Then I felt a second finger sneak inside, just barely, but enough to stretch me further.

"Fuck, Gabe."

He didn't respond.

His teeth scraped my skin and I jerked.

"Are you okay? What happened?" he asked, sheer panic in his eyes.

I grinned and pointed at my teeth.

"Sorry," he said, then bit his bottom lip.

He just couldn't get any cuter.

I grabbed his hair again, gripped it like I was going to pull him up, then pressed him back down on my cock. He gagged, but didn't pull back this time, just dove again and shoved his second finger inside me, twisting as he pressed. He swallowed and spat, bobbed up and down, over and over.

I was *so* close.

He must've felt my abs tense because he let me fall from his mouth and slowly pulled his fingers out. My eyes opened and found his as he lifted my leg and shuffled around to face me, placing it on his shoulder.

"Condom?" I asked.

Panic shot through his eyes again.

"Stay here," I said as I flew off the bed. I kept one condom in my wallet for emergencies.

His eyes held a hint of suspicion when I returned, but he didn't say anything, just watched as I tore open the packet with my teeth. He twitched as I rolled the rubber onto his dick.

I laid on my back again, and he lifted my legs to his shoulders. He squirted lube onto himself.

Before he could set the bottle down, I said, "Can you put some down there too? You're not exactly small yourself."

Fingers painted my hole and inner cheeks with warmth and slickness, then everything froze.

He was staring at me. I held his gaze, then asked, "Everything okay?"

He nodded slowly. "Just taking a picture of something very special."

Dammit, I giggled. I fucking giggled right there before . . .

He didn't let me finish that thought. His unpracticed hips slammed his cock inside me so fast, I nearly screamed for mercy. Fire lanced my ass and spine, but I saw such need in his eyes that I knew I couldn't ask him to stop. I sucked up the pain, gripped his pillows, and closed my eyes as he thrust into me again and again. By the fifth—or twentieth—I had relaxed and was begging for him to drive deeper into me.

It had been years since I'd let anyone inside me. He wasn't as big as me, but his cock was thick. God, it felt good.

He didn't last long. One, maybe two minutes after that first excruciating lunge, I felt his whole body quake and his thrusts quicken. He made to pull out, but I gripped his hip and forced him to spend himself inside me, then keep shoving until the last of his load filled the condom. He slipped out and flopped over next to me, his head resting on my shoulder.

"That felt so . . . Ty . . . wow."

I chuckled and kissed his forehead.

He bolted upright. "You didn't . . . I mean, should I . . . I'm sorry—"

I pressed a finger to his lips. "Last night, this morning, they were all about you, remember? Besides, I got exactly what I wanted."

He stared a moment, probably trying to guess if I was just being nice, then leaned down and kissed me with the tenderness I'd only seen when

. . .

He rolled onto his back again.

Faded images of my mom drifted through my mind. She was chopping onions. My dad came up behind her, gently gripped her hand holding the knife, and laid it down. She spun around and their lips pressed together. They hadn't seen me watching from the hallway. I was only six or seven. The gentleness and depth in that embrace, in that kiss, engraved itself on my heart. I felt it every time I thought of her. I felt it whenever someone got close to me.

And then I felt her loss and the emptiness it left inside me.

Gabe's eyes were closed, and his breathing was steady. I tried to untangle my arm without waking him, but his eyes flew open.

"Going somewhere?"

I kissed his forehead. "Thought I heard the washer. I'll go toss my shirt into the dryer."

He glanced down at his messy body and the condom still clinging to the end of his now-limp dick. "Guess I should shower. Join me if you like."

I nodded absently and kissed him again, then vanished into the safety of the laundry room.

Chapter 25

GABE

We pulled into the driveway of a cute East Nashville bungalow and parked behind a blue and white police cruiser. The house's white siding was offset by caramel shutters, and flower boxes the precise width of the window held rich autumn-colored flowers. Several pumpkins and gourds lay scattered between two rocking chairs and the front door.

Ty glanced over at me before getting out of his truck. "They moved in together about four months ago. You'd think two lesbians took over for all the work they've been doing to the place."

"It looks more like Martha Stewart than Rosie O'Donnell," I quipped.

He chuckled. "Tell me that after you see inside."

The front door opening turned both our heads, and a tall, beefy man in a white Nashville Predators T-shirt stepped onto the porch and waved. I thought I smiled a lot, but his nearly reached his ears.

"That's Miguel. Before you ask, yes, he's *always* smiling. You'll get used to it."

Ty opened the door and let the dogs out. They raced past Miguel and into the house like they owned the place. Miguel tried to pet Audie as she streaked by, but she ducked and chased after Dom.

We'd barely made it out of the truck and onto the first step of the porch before Miguel reached down and lifted Ty off the ground and into a bear hug.

Holy cow, Miguel's strong, and Ty's a big guy himself.

They exchanged pats on the back, and I was sure each said something, but their lips were obscured. Ty turned to me with a raised brow and a question in his eyes.

I shrugged and shook my head.

"Oh shit. Sorry." He half-turned to Miguel. "He reads lips and has to see us to understand."

Miguel nodded.

"I asked if you wanted some of this hug action. Miguel might be a big bad cop, but he's a real softie." Ty patted Miguel's stomach, and I worried he might've bruised his palm against the man's abs.

I started to tell them I was fine and hugs weren't necessary, but Miguel bounded down the steps, scooped me up, and spun me so my legs dangled and flew into the air. I let out a cry, and I could feel his laughter rumbling through his chest and into mine. There was such joy in his vibrations, I couldn't help but add my own giggles.

On one of the twirls, I caught a glimpse of Ty. He was all teeth and wide eyes.

Miguel set me down suddenly and turned toward the door. Another man, this one in shorts and an apron that read ~~Kiss~~ Lick the Cook stood with his fists on his hips. One hand reached up and waved a wooden spoon I hadn't seen.

"... you two alone for one minute and look what happens," was all I caught as my feet hit the ground.

My aproned savior stepped forward, stuffed the spoon into an apron pocket, and extended a meaty palm. "I'm Sam. Ignore whatever these mongrels said or did out here. Come to think of it, please forgive this one"—he hooked a thumb toward Ty—"for *anything* he's *ever* done. I swear, I told him not to do it, whatever it was."

Ty was chuckling when my eyes darted toward him. "This is Sam."

I looked back, climbed the first step, and gripped Sam's hand. It was like shaking an iron vice. "It's nice to finally meet you. Ty says—"

"Ty talks shit. Don't believe a word out of his mouth."

I giggled. "He says really nice things about you."

Sam didn't flinch. "Like I said, don't believe a word." Then he winked. "Now, you two, come inside and grab a beer. Gabe, ignore the mess. We're still fixing up the place."

He started to turn, then looked over my shoulder. "Babe, make sure Ty behaves while I'm cooking, okay?"

"Hey!" Ty feigned protest, then reached out and placed his hand on my shoulder, guiding me toward the door. As we reached Sam, he tapped so I would look back at him. "I'll keep you safe. Just stay close."

I giggled, and pressed his forehead into mine.

Sam eyed Ty, then looked toward me, then behind me to Miguel. Some invisible communication took place in that gaze, and his smile broadened as he turned to go back inside.

Ty hadn't been wrong about the whole lesbian vibe. When we walked in, the scent of fresh paint, drywall, and some kind of glue slammed into me. The foyer looked complete, and was immaculate. Crisply painted mustard walls were offset by the rich wood of antique furniture. A wooden mantle above the brick hearth on the near wall held framed photos of Sam and Miguel, individually and together. One of Miguel in his uniform jumped out at me, and I walked over to take a closer look.

Ty stepped around to face me. "He's really handsome in his uniform, isn't he?"

I nodded. "They both are."

"Don't tell them I said this, but they were made for each other. Regular bookends. Just wait until you see them in action. It's like watching twins or some odd conjoined aliens who share the same brain. I knew the first time I saw them together at the shop they'd end up dating. I hadn't expected wedding bells."

"Wedding?"

He nodded. "Miguel proposed the month before they bought this place, said he didn't feel right moving in unless Sam was his fiancé. If I had a heart, I'd think that was sweet or something."

I giggled and shoved him. The beast didn't budge.

He leaned over and kissed my cheek.

Ty's head whipped up, and I turned to see Miguel finishing some smart-ass remark. Ty looked toward me. "He said we weren't allowed to show PDA in his house, that this was a Christian home."

I started to giggle, but Ty's tongue cut me off. Before I could protest, he'd wrapped his arms around me and lifted me off the ground again.

I pretended to be mad. "You two really need to stop picking me up."

The beasts just laughed.

Thankfully, one beast was still loyal—at least, I thought Audie was being loyal when she rounded the corner. The fickle furball ignored me and leapt up, planted her front paws on Ty's chest, and proceeded to lick his face. I regained some sense of self-worth when Dom, trailing on her heels, knocked me back onto a couch and slobbered all over my cheek.

By the time we had the dogs under control, Sam had snuck around the corner and was peering over Miguel's shoulder. Both of them wore self-satisfied grins I thought implied more than I understood.

This was beginning to feel like one of those family reunions where distant relatives exchange knowing glances, but left me out of the telepathy department.

"Let's go out back. I'll be done with lunch in a few," Sam said before kissing Miguel's neck.

We followed the guys through the dining room, into the kitchen, then out onto the back patio. The dogs ran by, excited by the presence of a few squirrels at the far end of the fenced-in yard.

Sam flipped steaks at a small grill while the three of us settled into chairs at a round table shaded by a salmon-colored umbrella. Ty surprised me by taking my hand in his and holding it while we waited for lunch.

As silly as it sounds, I was thankful for the table's shape because it forced everyone to face each other, making it much easier to lipread without having to constantly remind the hearing folks to turn toward me. I was used to it, but hated having to think about things like that all the time.

Over steaks, baked potatoes, and beer, we chatted about everything and nothing. Ty peppered Sam and Miguel about wedding plans, and I giggled incessantly as they made googly eyes at each other. Ty teased them for setting a date nearly a year into the future, accusing the guys of giving themselves time to change their minds before tying the knot. Sam rolled his eyes and waved him off, explaining how their plate was full fixing up the house, and the wedding deserved their complete attention when its time came. He grabbed Miguel's neck and pulled him into a kiss.

When Miguel freed himself, he grinned and said, "It would take an asteroid hitting the earth to stop us from getting married. Miguel's never getting away from me—I have handcuffs, after all."

We all laughed, and another wave raced up my arm as Ty squeezed my hand.

There was so much love in that house.

Ty took a bite, and Miguel seized the opportunity to ask about how we'd met. I had the feeling he already knew the story but wanted to hear how we retold it.

Once a cop, always a cop, I thought.

And so the afternoon went.

The dogs eventually wore out and curled up together at our feet. The four of us ate, drank, and chatted like we'd known each other for a lifetime. A few times, Sam forgot I couldn't hear him, but Miguel spun him around to repeat whatever he'd said to the others before either Ty or I could say a word. The guys clearly loved Ty, and by the end of the day, I knew they'd welcomed me into their fold with open arms.

I left Ty's condo later that evening. Audie slept soundly in the back seat. My stomach was full, and my heart was bursting at the seams.

Chapter 26

TYLER

Whoever said "time flies" wasn't lying.

It felt like yesterday that I was still in Pensacola, standing by my dad as he took his new wife-to-be's hand. At nineteen, I wouldn't say I was innocent, but I certainly was young.

As the sun rose and Dom licked me awake on my thirtieth birthday, the weight of those intervening years settled onto my shoulders. It might sound silly. Thirty was still young. It's the perfect age, actually. People start taking you seriously, but don't expect too much because you're still too young to know a lot. Age had never bothered me before. Then again, when did age ever bother the young? They're too stupid to know what growing up really means. We all are—until we wake up one day, all grown up, and reality dumps a turd in our lap.

I'd been around dogs too long.

Life rarely dropped turds, especially in the morning.

Dom had actually let me sleep until seven. I took that as further evidence on the life-morning-poop argument.

We did our morning thing, then piled into my truck and headed to the dog park. I had to get rid of Dom's excess energy before cleaning up and heading over to Sam and Miguel's. I'd made Sam promise not to throw some annoying surprise party, but Miguel had refused to take part in our foolish party poopery, as he called it. It was plain something was up, and it was going to be huge—or painful—or both, if I knew Sam and Miguel at all.

My Spidey sense was further triggered when my erstwhile boyfriend refused to sleep over the night of my birth. Gabe giggled and feigned innocence, but he was the worst liar in the history of lying.

It had been a few months since our eyes had met across a crowded coffee shop, and I'd finally admitted he made me crazy. We'd fallen into a comfortable routine, meeting at the dog part every day after work, then having dinner together and flipping a coin over whose place we'd sleep at. I think we slept apart twice in all that time. The idea of spending time apart was beginning to bother me; like, *really* bother me. I hated when he wasn't there, when I couldn't smell him on my pillowcase, when I didn't wake to his smile or heartbeat or steady breath. His head belonged on my shoulder, with the rest of him pressed snugly against me.

I couldn't explain what had changed.

I'd been a perfectly happy party boy with an endless stream of hookups at my beck and call. I loved the party scene; craved it. Workweeks were nothing more than a conduit to the next weekend of drug-enhanced dancing and sex. I might've been blessed with good genetics, but I'd worked hard for years to have a body other guys craved. The parties filled more than just sexual desires, they fed my ego and affirmed my worth. Every time guys fell over themselves, I knew I was really wanted.

At least, that's what I thought I knew. That's how it felt. I never stopped to question or doubt it. Who questioned a good time?

Then along came this floppy haired, dimpled deaf dude.

He messed *everything* up.

And I was falling in love with him for it.

Just the thought of him made my heart beat a little faster. He had a light inside him, a way about him, that made everyone around him—including me, *especially* me—happier and better for his presence. It made no sense. All he did was smile or giggle and I turned into some unintelligent puddle of mush.

What the fuck?

I was a strappin' hot fucker with muscles and a cockiness that . . . that fucking fell apart when Gabe entered a room.

Nobody had ever—

A knock on my truck's window, immediately followed by two sharp barks, interrupted my thoughts.

"You coming in or just sitting out here all day?" Sam cocked his head. He was back in his apron and wielding his spoon-sword weapon at my truck. Gabe's car was in the driveway, along with Miguel's cruiser, but that was it.

Huh. Some surprise party. Maybe they actually listened to me for once.

Upbeat music drifted through the door as we approached, but I couldn't hear any voices or anything else that might indicate hijinks, just Audie's occasional bark from somewhere deep in the house. I glanced back at Sam.

"What? Go on. Lunch'll get cold if we stand out here all day."

I turned back and opened the door. Dom ran in right before a chorus of "Happy birthday!" rang out. Miguel and Gabe stood in front of a couple dozen other people. Everyone clapped and laughed at the surprised look on my face as Sam wrapped his arm around my shoulder.

"Happy birthday, buddy."

For once, I didn't make a smart remark or shy from his touch, just reached across and hugged him back as a lump found its way into my throat. He was family, after all.

The house, almost fully remodeled, was covered in silver and gold streamers and balloons. I turned back to the waiting pack to find most faces I recognized: Miguel's partner Donna, Annie, the Broadway singer who owned seats in front of Miguel at the Sounds stadium and had practically adopted him a few years back, and several of the guys from the shop.

Behind Gabe stood another group who waved their hands in the air when everyone else clapped. I'd never met his friends, but picked out Lucas and Bryan right away. Something in their presence sent a thrill of both excitement and terror through me.

What if they don't like me? What if they think I'm not good enough for Gabe? What if—

"Ty." Gabe's voice snapped me out of my mental flagellation. "This is Bryan."

I knew two things about Bryan from Gabe's stories. First, he was flamboyant to the point of flaming; and second, he looked seventeen on a good day, even though he was actually twenty-two. Oh, a third thing I'd forgotten: Bryan didn't lipread or talk well.

Awesome awkwardness, Batman.

The platinum-haired teenager stepped past my outstretched palm and, without warning, pulled me toward him and kissed me on the mouth. His eyes widened as he squeezed my biceps, then let go and fell back behind Gabe. I was so stunned, I'd barely closed my mouth before Gabe's giggle burst out. My eyes darted around to find everyone laughing, a few with tears in their eyes. I must've been pale as a sheet—or brilliant crimson.

But one man wasn't laughing.

He stood about shoulder height to me, but loomed over Gabe's shoulder. There was no moisture in his eyes, and his mouth was definitely not turned upward. In fact, he looked on the verge of misery.

"And this is Lucas," Gabe said through gasps, pointing behind him with an open palm.

Lucas glowered as I stepped forward and held out my hand. Reluctantly, he reached up, shook, and released it so fast I'd barely felt his touch at all. Then his fingers moved faster than I'd thought was possible.

I turned my blank stare to Gabe.

His wide grin had turned into a thin line.

"He says he's happy to meet you, and wishes you a happy birthday."

Lucas fired off another round of signs, each looking sharper and angrier than the last.

I might not've known what words he was forming, but the emotions conveyed in his communications were clear. A couple others in the deaf group who Gabe hadn't had time to introduce grabbed Lucas by his elbows and pulled him away toward the kitchen, leaving Bryan, Gabe, and me staring blankly at each other.

Bryan rubbed a closed fist in circles over the center of his chest and mouthed, "Sorry."

"He says—"

"I got that. Tell him thanks."

I watched him form a few signs, then turn back to me. He continued signing as he spoke, "Let's go get something to drink. Whatever Sam cooked smells amazing too. Come on."

Bryan and I followed him back through the kitchen to the patio, where most of the partygoers had drifted. One handed me a beer and clapped me on the shoulder. I glanced up, surprised to see Marcus.

"Hey," I said, completely thrown off by, well, everything the day had given me so far. "What are you—"

"Sam posted online about the party. I reached out and asked if I could attend."

"Oh, okay," I said, still stunned. "Thanks."

He leaned in. "Why don't I send you into your thirties with a much better party later?"

"Wha—? Oh . . . wow . . . shit . . . I—"

Marcus walked fingers up my chest and whispered, "Let me know before I leave. I got some good stuff, and my ass really misses you." Then he kissed my cheek and turned away.

I'd barely remembered to close my mouth before Gabe's hand pressed into my back.

"Who was that?" he asked.

"Oh, nobody. Just some guy—"

I glanced up to find Lucas glaring at me.

I gripped Gabe's arms and kissed his lips. "He's nobody. Just an old friend I haven't seen in a while. I was surprised he was here. That's all."

Gabe shrugged. "Okay. I was just curious when you didn't introduce us. Let's go get something to eat."

I sucked in a breath, took Gabe's hand, and let him pull me to a table by the grill. Bryan followed a step behind. I glanced back and caught his eye. His previous good humor was still there, but something else, something unsettling, swam in his gaze.

As parties went, this one was tame. Sam had set up corn hole in the yard, but the dogs kept stealing the beanbags and running into the house. After a few trips to retrieve them, we gave up and let the dogs have their fun. The shop guys huddled near the grill where Sam cooked throughout the day. Miguel held court with his cadre, and the deaf guys sat around the table and signed quietly.

The phrase "signed quietly" made me chuckle. There wasn't really a loud way to sign, though I supposed some of the slappier motions made sounds. Gabe had taught me that deaf people equated all their communication to how hearing people spoke. They didn't watch someone sign. They *listened*. They didn't see words. They *heard* them. When two people engaged in an ASL conversation, they weren't signing, they were *talking*.

While Gabe didn't seem bothered when one of us mixed up the verbiage, he'd warned me that others in his community took great offense to the wrong term. They equated it to hearing people thinking less of their method of communicating, looking down on them. I didn't understand how that made sense, but accepted it at face value when he'd explained it.

It was sad to me that most of his friends couldn't communicate in ways other than ASL. Some lipread. A few others, like Gabe and Lucas, spoke well and lipread, but most lived in their silent cocoon amid the flowering world of sound.

At one point in the afternoon, Sam and Miguel had Gabe cornered and were picking his brain about puppy breeds they should consider. They had their own highly personal language when it came to that subject. They weren't adopting a dog, they were growing their family. As one adopted by a furry beast, I got it, but they still cracked me up. Sam had come a long way since our early years in Nashville. Miguel had more to do with that metamorphosis than anyone. I smiled as they peppered poor Gabe with question after question.

"Do you love him?"

I nearly dropped my beer.

I turned and found myself face-to-face with Lucas.

"I asked, do you love him?" His jaw was set, his voice stern. He didn't have the clear diction I'd come to enjoy from Gabe, but I understood both his words and their underlying meaning. This was Gabe's protector sniffing out a potential threat.

"I really like him a lot, yeah."

"That's not the same thing." He crossed his arms and motioned with his head for me to sit at the table. Any hint of Bryan's prior smile was gone as he and two others of their group bore lasers into me. Lucas signed as he spoke. "Here's the deal, birthday boy. Our friend, a man I happen to love more than life itself, is falling in love with you. Hell, he's already in love with you. If you can't see that, you're dumber than I thought before."

I started to open my mouth, but he kept going.

"What I want to know is if you love him, or is this just another one of your parties? Once the drugs wear off, will you just go back home to whatever city you flew in from?"

My eyes widened. I glanced around the table, but the others remained silent, their eyes pinned to me.

"Lucas, Gabe is incredible. I love being with him. When he's not with me, I . . . I—"

"You what?"

"I miss him. He's so special, more special than anyone I've ever dated. I mean, I've never really dated, but, you know what I mean."

One brow raised, but he remained silent. The others had their arms cross when I peeked away.

"I don't know what you want me to say."

"What do you think is best for Gabe?" he asked.

"What's best . . . what . . . I don't understand."

"Do you ever wonder how he feels living in your world?"

"My world?"

"Let me finish." He held up a palm. "Gabe is deaf. Tomorrow, he'll be deaf. Twenty years from now, he'll still be deaf. Every time you turn your back to him, he'll be deaf. Every time you bring him to a party with all your hearing friends who don't know to face him, he'll be deaf."

"I know—"

"And he'll feel alone."

That stopped whatever I was going to say. The thought of Gabe being alone tore at my heart. All at once, I felt it rip, like nothing I'd felt since—

"The more he integrates into your world, the more he leaves ours—*his*. Who will he have, who will he turn to, when he is alone? When he is lonely? Who will understand?"

"I'll be there," I began weakly.

Lucas shook his head, as if a child had answered. "Do you know how to sign? Have you even learned one sign since you've been with Gabe?"

I thought a moment, then tried to sign his name, the *G* over my heart. I accidentally used two fingers, forming an *H.*

"In all this time, you haven't even bothered to learn his name." When Lucas stood, the others rose. "I think you answered my question. Thank you . . . and happy birthday."

Without another word or glance toward Gabe, they walked through the house and left.

Chapter 27

GABE

I glanced up from puppy talk with Sam and Miguel to find Ty sitting at the table by himself. At first, I thought Lucas and the others must've gone inside. The sun was starting to set and it was getting cooler outside. Luc could be a delicate flower sometimes. Then I noticed the set of Tyler's shoulders, how they slumped, and I knew something was wrong.

"Guys, give me a minute, okay?"

Sam and Miguel exchanged a confused look and nodded. I could feel their eyes following me as I moved to the table and placed a hand on Ty's shoulder.

"Hey, you okay?"

His head snapped up.

"Fine. I'm good. Yeah. Fine."

I sat and waited. He didn't speak again. He didn't even look at me.

I reached for his forearm, but he pulled away, resting his hand in his lap.

"Ty, what happened? Talk to me."

"Are you lonely?"

"What? No, of course not."

Where had that come from?

"Are you sure? Even when you can't hear me?"

Ah. Of course. "Ty, what did Lucas say to you?"

His head hung. I had to turn his chin toward me to see his lips. When our eyes met, my heart lurched.

"Please talk to me, Tyler. What's going on?"

"I'm sorry, Gabe. I . . . I need to think, alright? I just need to think." He stood and darted into the house. By the time Sam and Miguel sat with me, he'd leashed Dom and left.

"What was all that?" Sam asked.

"I'm not sure, but I'm going to find out. Can you watch Audie for me?"

"Of course, but what—"

I stood, then leaned over and hugged them in turn. "Thanks for a great party, guys. I know he loved it. I'll be back."

Chapter 28

GABE

I sat in Sam's driveway for a long moment, then grabbed my phone to see if Ty had texted. There were no messages waiting. Anger bubbled inside me. I let my fingers fly.

ME: WHERE ARE YOU? WHAT THE HELL DID YOU SAY TO TYLER?

A long moment passed, then the dots danced, then stopped, then danced again.

LUC: WE'RE AT MY CONDO, ALL OF US ARE.

Me: I'm on my way.

I knew Bry was there with them, but I had to know what I was walking into.

Me: Do you know what Luc said to Ty? Talk to me. How pissed should I be?

Bryan: I think you should hear Luc out before you decide how you feel.

Me: What the hell, Bry? Really?

He didn't text back, didn't bother to give me a heads-up on the ambush that lay in wait for me—in plain sight.

I tried to breathe slowly, to calm myself, but the longer I sat still in that car, the angrier I got. Tyler didn't deserve whatever guilt trip they'd laid on him, and if anyone knew guilt, it was Luc. He didn't just have guilt, he rolled around in it, smeared it on his face, drank it in. I loved him like an older brother, but he took the ills of the world on his shoulders and wore them like a mantle. Martyr barely described him some days.

This was clearly one of those days, and I planned to take him down a few pegs for it.

I didn't knock when I got to his place. I stormed in. Fury was my cloak.

Four faces stared up at me. They sat in a circle in Luc's den. Bryan was across from me in a La-Z-Boy. Kevin and Steven sat on the couch. Luc sat nearest me in a kitchen chair he'd pulled over to form the circle. Another kitchen chair sat empty next to the television.

No one spoke for the longest time.

Finally, Luc motioned to the chair. I thought about remaining on my feet in a petty act of defiance, but reason told me it wouldn't change anything, so I sat.

Luc began signing without moving his lips, forcing me into his world of silent speech.

"I'm sorry Tyler was upset, but it was important we had a conversation with him."

"What conversation?" I spoke aloud, forcing Luc to interpret for the others.

"I asked if he loves you."

"What? Really?" If I'd been walking just then, I would've stumbled. My voice shrank as I asked, "What did he say?"

Luc blew out a breath. "He said he really likes you."

My heart froze.

"Gabe, I know you're falling for Ty, but please, hear me out. Hear *us* out. We love you, and we're not the ones afraid to say so."

My mouth wouldn't move. I had to remind myself to breathe. I felt something inside me snap, and I nodded numbly as I locked my legs together beneath the chair.

"Gabe, let's set aside the communication challenges between a hearing and a deaf partner. There's no need to beat those into the ground. Besides, they're not what concerns me most here."

I cocked my head. I would've put good money on that being his issue. He was all about waving the deaf flag in someone's face. What could possibly trump that?

"It's Tyler himself."

"What about—?"

He silenced me with a sharp look. "Gabe, he's a party boy. He's always been one, always will be. Did you see him there with that guy? I watched them. They were a lot more than casual friends."

"I know about Ty's past."

"What if it's not his past?"

I blinked. Tyler had been with me for months. We'd been together nearly every night. I knew that wasn't . . . I was sure . . .

"Has he told you about Las Vegas?"Now I was perplexed.

"What about Las Vegas?"

"There's another circuit party there in November. Tyler has tickets."

"How could you know that?"

Luc leaned forward. "Because I know some of the same people he sees at his club. The Shadow Box was his favorite, right?"

I was speechless.

"He has tickets to Vegas. I don't know if he's bought his flight yet, but he also has a room in one of the hotels on the strip. He bought it, along with a block of other guys. They got a group rate for doing it together."

"I . . . I don't know. Maybe he was—"

"Maybe he was what? Planning to take you with him? Are you into drugs and mindless orgies too now?"

"No, of course not. I just—"

"You're just grasping for the Tyler you think you know, Gabe. That's not who this guy is." Luc drew in a breath and held it. When he signed again, his movements were smoother, calmer. "You're my best friend in the world. The last thing I would ever want is to hurt you, but you need to know what you're doing here."

My eyes fell to my hands. When I didn't respond, he pressed forward, speaking and signing.

"Add to all that, I'm not sure I believe him when he says he really cares about you."

My head snapped up, and the anger that had ebbed flared to life again.

"Easy," Luc said. "Has he once asked to meet your friends?"

I thought a moment. "No, not in so many words."

"Has he asked to learn more about the deaf community? Has he shown an interest in our events or learning more about the challenges we face?"

I crossed my arms. "We've talked about it some."

"Has he asked you to teach him any signs? Maybe a few simple ones? Everybody wants to know how to curse in another language. It's fun."

"No . . . well . . . I taught him my name."

"Yeah, he tried to show that to me." He sat back.

"What do you mean?""He even got that wrong." He held up an *H* to mock what Ty had done. My heart sank. Not being able to sign wasn't a big deal, but forgetting the one thing I'd taught him? Forgetting my name? Something about that stabbed at my gut.

When I looked back up, Luc leaned over and took my hand, effectively shutting the others out of what he would ask next.

"Does he know what could happen? What might happen with your vision? What about your balance?"

I'd never even thought to talk about some of those possibilities. Usher was categorized into three types. Type one was primarily noted by severe hearing loss or deafness, as well as balance problems at birth. Many saw degradation of night vision, progressing to severe vision loss by midlife. For those with type two, hearing loss at birth ranged between moderate to severe, but without balance issues. Vision regression occurred in largely the same way as type one. People with type three Usher—*my* class—may experience no hearing impairment at birth, but lose their hearing gradually throughout adolescence. Vision loss and balance issues vary with the individual. Some never experience problems, while others find themselves in their forties and wobbling or straining to see for the first time.

The doctors had no idea how my Usher would progress as I grew older, but, at the ripe old age of twenty-seven, my vision was still twenty-twenty, and I had the balance of a cat. I rarely gave Usher much thought. The damage it had done to my hearing was embedded in who I was now, but the syndrome otherwise didn't impact my life.

"No."

Luc cocked his head. "No what?"

"No, I haven't told him about the other possibilities. I honestly didn't think about them."

His features softened. "It's a lot, I know." He looked around at the group, then resumed signing. "It's a lot for all of us, but we're here, Gabe. We're here for you, no matter what, and we always will be. Are you sure you can say the same about Tyler? Will he stand by you, support you, *see* and *hear* for you? Or will he run off to Las Vegas like old times?""That's not fair—"

"No, none of this is fair. You're right, and I'm more sorry than you could ever know to cause you pain. I love—*we* love—seeing you happy. We want you to be happy, but Tyler . . ."

He never finished his sentence.

No one spoke after that.

The car ride to get Audie, then home, felt like the longest trip of my life.

Chapter 29

TYLER

I knew what whiplash felt like, that sickening sensation of being jerked one way suddenly as the world around you lurched in the other direction.

God, it hurt.

I had no idea what was happening to Gabe and me, but it felt like a seismic shift. Every sense in my body cried out to text or call him. For some reason, I didn't.

I don't know why.

My phone was right there on the couch. I knew it was charged because it was plugged in. There was no reason not to reach out, to try and fix whatever had broken—*if* something had broken. I didn't even know that.

Then Luc's words assaulted my mind. His question, over and over.

Do you love him?

Who the hell was he to ask that? Whatever I felt for Gabe was between us. It was private. I wasn't about to use the *L* word with one of his friends before I used it with Gabe. That would've been wrong, wouldn't it?

Should I have just said whatever he wanted to hear?

Should I have told him I was madly in love with Gabe just to shut his arrogant ass up?

Was I in love with Gabe?

My head fell onto the back of the couch and I stared up at the ceiling, not seeing anything. There had been more to Lucas's questions. He knew things, or he thought he did. What wasn't he saying? What were the questions beneath his questions?

I could feel something bigger there, just beneath the surface, but my heart ached too much to grasp anything other than how much I missed Gabe.

How could one person miss another so much when they weren't even gone?

Was he gone?

I grabbed my phone and texted.

ME: HEY, YOU.

Nothing. Not even read. Just delivered.

I waited until my phone said ten minutes had passed.

ME: HEY. YOU THERE?

Still nothing. Still just delivered.

I dropped my phone back on the couch.

Dom looked up from his bed and whimpered. He rose and padded over to me, then rested his head on my lap. I swear that dog sensed my moods better than any human ever could.

"Buddy, I think I fucked up, but I don't know how, and I don't know how to fix it either."

He whimpered again.

"Yeah, that about says it all."

Around nine o'clock, my phone chirped. I'd fallen asleep on the couch. Dom was settled back in his bed, but glanced up when I sat forward.

DEAF DIMPLES: I'M HERE. CAN WE TALK?

ME: TELL ME WHEN AND WHERE.

DEAF DIMPLES: COFFEE SHOP IN AN HOUR?

ME: SEE YOU THEN.

A rush of adrenaline raged through me, and I shouted at the ceiling. I wasn't sure if "Can we talk?" was a good thing or not, but there was nothing Gabe and I couldn't figure out together if we really tried. We were good like that.

Too anxious to sit around my condo, I tossed Dom a Greenie and ran to my truck. Ten minutes and three traffic violations later, I sat at a table in the corner of Buddy Brew, java in hand, staring intently at the door.

Thirty minutes and two coffees later, I was still twenty minutes early. The door chime rang and my head snapped up to see Marcus stride in. He wore a painted-on firetruck-red club top and even tighter jeans that revealed just how far to the left he really hung. I looked down, desperate to avoid his gaze.

He approached the counter without seeing me. I sucked in a breath of relief.

"Hey, sexy." Marcus's hand massaged my shoulder.

I looked up. "Hey, Marcus.

"Why so down? You look like somebody shot your dog." Panic shot through him. "Your dog—"

"Dom's fine. There's been no shooting."

"Oh god, thank you. I was about to feel like an ass." He scooted a chair around to sit beside me and ran a hand across my leg. "Speaking of ass . . ."

"Marcus, I really can't, not anymore."

His brows shot upward. "Oh?"

"I'm, well, kind of seeing someone."

His hand retreated and he sat back. "No shit. Really?"

I nodded. "I really like this guy. I think it's serious."

"Wow. Good for you, Ty. Is he into three-ways? I could totally squeeze in between—"

"No. Just . . . just no."

"Okay." He held up both palms in surrender. "Can't blame a whore for asking."

"Come on, Marcus, you know whores get paid."

It was an oldie, but a goodie. We both laughed. Just then, the barista called out his name. Marcus leaned over, gave me a peck on the temple, and stepped away.

"He's a lucky guy, Ty. You're a hot fuck."

I saluted with my coffee cup. "Thanks."

Motion near the door drew my eye. Gabe was standing there, watching.

I stood and waved. "Hey, how long—"

The door slammed behind him.

Chapter 30

TYLER

I'd forgotten about Vegas. Gabe had helped me forget about a lot of things.

He wouldn't respond to my texts after that night in the coffee shop. I tried. I even showed up one Friday night when the deaf group was there. Gabe avoided my eyes, and Lucas gave me a dark glare. My old pal, Woody, warned me away from troubled waters, as he called it, so I left.

Dom and I went to the dog park every evening after work. He searched for Audie. I stared at the double gate, hoping Gabe would walk through it. Neither did.

Sam and Miguel said they didn't know any more than I did, but I suspected they were just trying to protect me. From what, I didn't know. I guess

I was glad for that. They were my family and, if they thought I needed protecting, they were probably right. By the third week, I'd stopped asking them questions.

It was early November, two months after Gabe vanished from my life, when I ran across the party tickets in a cigar box on an end table in my den. I kept pens and paper in there, in case some note demanded scribbling, but I wasn't much of a scribbler, so it had gone undisturbed.

I sat on the couch and stared at the tickets.

Not that long ago, the sight of those golden slips would've rocked my world with visions of shirtless men, disco balls, and pills embossed with Superman's crest. Sitting there in my den, they felt like cold, lifeless pieces of paper.

Dom growled.

I glanced over.

His head cocked.

"Yeah, you're right. Daddy needs to snap out of it. You've been paying for my funk, and it's time we both moved on. Thanks, buddy."

He barked once.

I grabbed my phone and texted.

> **ME:** HEY. SORRY TO VANISH LIKE THAT.
> YOU STILL UP FOR WHATEVER?

Barely a second passed.

MARCUS: FOR THE HOTTEST FUCK IN NASHVILLE? HELL YEAH. WHATEVER, WHENEVER.

ME: SWEET. I HAVE AN IDEA.

MARCUS: OH SHIT. IT SCARES ME WHEN YOU THINK.

ME: HA HA. YOU SOUND LIKE MY BEST FRIEND. HE'S AN ASS TOO. ARE YOU GOING TO VEGAS?

MARCUS: DUDE, REALLY? ARE YOU SERIOUSLY ASKING ME THAT? OF COURSE I AM.

ME: PERFECT. HOW ABOUT YOU BE MY BOYFRIEND FOR THE WEEKEND?

There was a pause.

MARCUS: WTF?

ME: HEAR ME OUT. NOTHING SERIOUS. WE JUST PRETEND TO BE BOYFRIENDS FOR THE WEEKEND. WE DANCE TOGETHER, WE FLY TOGETHER, WE FUCK TOGETHER. IF WE FIND OTHERS, WE DO WHATEVER, BUT WE DO IT TOGETHER. THINK OF IT LIKE A WEEKEND-LONG ROLE PLAY.

MARCUS: WELL, SHIT. I GET TO STICK TO YOU ALL WEEKEND AND DO WHATEVER YOU DO, WITH YOU?

ME: YEP. THAT'S THE BOYFRIEND THING.

MARCUS: BUY ME A RING AND SLAP ME SILLY, BOYFRIEND.

ME: It's just for the weekend though. Nothing serious. When we get home, everything goes back.

MARCUS: Ty, we're good. You know I don't want anything like that.

ME: Cool. Let me drop and book my flight.

MARCUS: Hugs and kisses, sweetie.

ME: Fuck off.

MARCUS: I plan to . . . in Vegas.

***

Vegas was insane. Guys from all over the world flocked to Sin City for this party, and the organizers spared no expense to make it worth the trip. Marcus got over his initial jitters about our little role play and hammed up the *boyfriend thing*, as he called it, inventing ridiculous new stories about how we got together for each new guy we met. My personal favorite involved him working as a paramedic and saving my life when I was seriously injured in a car crash. Somehow, lifesaving medicine involved a blow job in the back of an ambulance. I'm pretty sure our cover was blown with that one.

By the time the sun rose on the Friday night party, we were so high I couldn't remember much. We slept it off throughout the day, waking only to eat and pass out again. Saturday night's main event featured live singers and world-famous DJs. We danced until four in the morning, then stumbled back to our hotel room. An hour of ecstasy-enhanced sex later, we were spent and fell asleep in each other's arms.

Somewhere around eleven thirty Sunday morning, I woke. Marcus was still dead to the world, so I sat up on an elbow and watched him. He was a really handsome guy, and his body was sick, but the longer I stared, I realized his hair was cropped too short. It should've been longer, maybe curled a little. That would've highlighted his eyes and framed his face better.

Framed his face? What the fuck do I know about shit like that?

I chuckled at my own silliness.

Then my eyes roamed down his muscled arm. It was smooth and perfect, just like every other part of him. He was a living, breathing Ken doll on steroids. Don't get me wrong, it was a look that was the envy of pretty much every guy who saw him shirtless, straight or gay. Who wouldn't want to look like a magazine cover? But as I traced his arms with my fingers, careful not to touch and wake him, there were no scars, no scratches or imperfections. It was like some perfectly formed ceramic version of a man lay next to me.

I watched him sleep, took in the rise and fall of his chest, wondered what he dreamed as his eyes twitched beneath heavy lids. It was such a beautiful moment. So simple and pure.

And so empty.

When I looked at Marcus, I saw a sexy man, but nothing more. In that moment, I realized I didn't even know his last name or where he worked—or what he even did for work. I didn't know where he was from, where he grew up, if he had a dog or cat, if he even liked pets.

I knew nothing about this man.

And in the stillness of that instant, my heart ached again.

I wanted to be staring at Gabe, to be watching his chest rise and fall, to be wondering about his dreams. He was from Genoa, Italy. His last name was Rossi, and he had a mother and brother and father who trained dogs. He loved pasta and home-made ice cream, and, above all, he loved his dog, Audie. He was deaf, but didn't let it rule his life. He smiled and laughed and, dammit, he giggled.

And I loved him.

I fucking loved him.

Why did I have to realize all this now? When I was a world away and it was too late to do any-thing anyway?

Why hadn't I seen . . .

Why hadn't I just said . . .

Tears streamed down my face as I admitted it all to myself, as I blamed myself for losing the most amazing man in the world. He might not be made of porcelain, but he held more beauty in his slim body than all the men sleeping off their party in Vegas combined.

I didn't need any of them.

I didn't need Marcus.

I needed Gabe.

And I loved him.

Chapter 31

TYLER

"Who plans a wedding in December?"

"What are you talking about? December is magical. Everyone's happy, even the sad people like you." Sam's mouth quirked.

"Great. You made your wedding sound like a Disney musical and insulted me all in the same sentence. Brilliant."

"Isn't this the happiest place on earth, Ty?" He said in a singsong voice.

"Fuck you and your happiness." I laughed. "Now come here so I can straighten that bowtie. Inspector Gadget has a whole department making sure his tux is perfect. You're stuck with me."

"I'm screwed, aren't I?"

I chuckled. "I love you, brother. You know that, right?"

He froze as I fixed his tie.

"I know, Ty. I love you too. Are you okay?"

"I'm good. Just wanted you to hear it. I don't know if I've ever said it before. It's important."

He gaped at me. "What have you done with Tyler Hyatt? Is this some body snatcher thing? Do I need to call in FEMA, or some mad scientist with crazy hair?"

"Ha ha. Very funny." I dusted off his shoulders. "Guess Gabe was good for me, after all. He might not've been my happily ever after, but he cracked me open some."

"Come here. Let me fix that. My best man has to look good too." He reached up and grabbed my tie. "You're a great guy, Ty. Don't ever doubt that. You'll find your guy one of these days, then I'll be the one giving you sappy shit before you walk out to tie the knot."

Before I could protest, Sam pulled me into a tight embrace. "You're the best man I know, Sam Prescott. I love you, brother."

When he pulled pack, I reached up and wiped a tear before it could fall.

"Thanks a lot. You messed up my tie and made me cry. My makeup's probably ruined now."

"Makeup? Lord, you're not an actress, Ty. Pull yourself up by your jockstrap."

I laughed and fixed my tie again. "You got it. It's time."

Unlike most weddings I'd attended where the bride walked down the aisle to majestic music, Sam and Miguel chose to enter from the two opposite side doors at the front of the church. I trailed behind Sam, while Donna stood in for Miguel. She was positively stunning, with her hair pulled up in an elegant chignon, and she wore a flowing sapphire gown. I had no clue Miguel's rugged partner could transform into a fairytale princess. She was beautiful.

When we met in the middle before the officiant, Sam and Miguel faced each other and joined hands. Miguel looked like a million bucks in his tuxedo, and his smile . . . Damn, when his eyes locked onto Sam's, his smile lit up the whole place.

The ceremony was painless and quick, with the officiant making only a few remarks before turning things over to the guys to share vows they'd each spent months writing. I'd seen twenty iterations of Sam's, and knew Miguel had drafted no less than twice as many. Individually, they were great guys. Together, they were beyond amazing. If there was ever a living example of men who made each other better, they were it.

Once the rings were placed and the magical kiss laid, the four of us turned toward the guests. Blue uniforms interspersed with colorful dresses and dark suits on Miguel's side. I turned to see who'd come to support Sam and my heart seized.

There, sitting in the third row, was Gabe.

Everyone began applauding the presentation of the couple, but my hands wouldn't rise. I couldn't move. My gaze was fixed on one point, on one person.

Sam's elbow nudged me, and I turned to lead the procession off the dais. I couldn't help looking back one last time as we entered the rectory.

Gabe was staring at me too.

Chapter 32

GABE

S am and Miguel stood before a three-tiered cake covered in white icing and intricate pearly scrollwork. The baker's sense of humor was on full display, as the toppers were figurines of a burly mechanic who looked more like a lumberjack holding a wrench, and a sunglass-wearing cop in a *CHiPs* uniform from the seventies. They'd even included a plastic puppy, a miniature version of a golden retriever standing on hind legs.

They cut the cake, and Sam smeared icing all over Miguel's face as the rest of us held champagne flutes aloft and toasted the newlyweds. Miguel then got his revenge by kissing Sam and shaking his head back and forth, transferring a solid half of the icing onto his new husband.

Something in their unbridled joy renewed my spirit and gave me hope for a brighter future. If love like that existed, anything was possible.

Then I turned and ran headlong into Tyler.

He'd been standing a few feet behind me the whole time.

"You, uh . . . you look good," I said artfully as my eyes traveled up and down his tuxedo.

He grinned and fidgeted with his fingers. Nobody noticed fingers like us deaf folk.

Then he did the last thing I would've expected.

Without speaking, he signed, "You look great too."

My jaw must've been on the floor because his smile widened.

Then he signed, "I really happy to see your bash-ful again."

"Wait, what? My bashful?"

He did the sign again.

"No, that's bashful, not face."

"Sorry." His face flushed crimson. "I meant face. It's nice to see your face again."

I tried to hold back a smile. I really tried.

"When did you learn those signs?"

He shrugged like it was nothing, like everyone knew a few bits of ASL. "I met a kid who taught me some."

"A kid?"

"Yeah, his mom brought her car into the shop. I saw them signing and ended up chatting with them. Shirley, his mom, told me how lonely he'd been. His dad left a few years ago, and he's just now turning twelve."

My brows furrowed. "You learned signs from a kid you met at the garage whose dad—?"

"Well, yeah, we met there, but I've kind of become his unofficial big brother. He goes with me to the dog park most afternoons. It's kind of weird because he can't lipread very well, and I never signed before meeting him, but we're figuring it out. He's a great kid. His name's Ben."

Something in my chest twisted. Tyler was being a good guy. I couldn't take it.

"I need to go," I said, turning away.

His hand clamped around my arm, then released. "Please, have a glass of champagne with me . . . for Sam and Miguel."

Sneaky fucker. I rolled my eyes and motioned him toward the table with the full flutes. We grabbed our bubbly and headed to a table near the corner. A long, awkward moment passed as we sat and watched guests mill about. Ty glanced at me a couple times, but I kept my eyes away from his. No good would be had by eye contact.

"I've missed you."

My eyes flew to his. "Please tell me why. I'm intrigued."

He sucked in a breath. He really was nervous. This was going to be good.

"Lucas was right."

Well, that wasn't what I'd expected.

"He said I was, well, a lot of things, and he was right. I've spent my whole adult life running from anything that might tie me down or make me uncomfortable. Sam's the only person I've ever let get close to me. Until you. I wasn't boyfriend material. Hell, I might never be a good one, but I know I want to try. I know that now."

"What about that guy?"

"What guy?"

"The one I saw kiss you at the coffee shop. He was at your birthday party too. Marcus? I think that was his name."

"Marcus never was more than a hookup. I was waiting for you and he walked in for coffee. He tried to get me to go out with him that night, but I told him I couldn't."

"Why?"

He glanced down, then back up. "Because I was seeing someone."

My heart began to beat a little quicker, and breathing suddenly became a conscious choice.

"You said that to him?"

He nodded. "I left right after you did."

I wanted to crawl under the table. It didn't matter. None of that mattered. Sam was a playboy and there were too many—*far* too many—obstacles. It would never work.

"What about Las Vegas?" I asked.

His eyes widened.

Bingo.

"I bought tickets to that party last spring, before we met. I'd actually forgotten about it until a couple months after we . . . after things ended."

"But you still went?"

He nodded. "I don't know why. Someone told me to get back on the horse, that I was moping too much. I guess I thought . . . I don't know. That's all I've ever done. I didn't know how else to get back on my feet."

Wow. He'd really been torn up over us.

"I went to Vegas to get my mojo back, but it kind of backfired."

"Backfired? How?"

Ty rubbed his palms over his face, then swept his hair back. He stared at the table, then at his hands, then finally up at me.

"I kept seeing you, wishing you were there. Not *there*, not in Vegas. I didn't mean that. I mean . .

. shit . . . I wished I was with you. I was standing in a sea of the most ridiculously hot men anywhere on the planet, and all I could think was that none of them compared to you."

I wanted to be flattered. God, I wanted to believe him and think I could be in his league for just a minute, but that seemed so unrealistic. What's that phrase about something that sounds too good to be true?

I decided it was time to drop my bomb and watch him flee for the countryside—or bar—whichever worked for him.

"I might lose my sight . . . and my balance."

He bolted upright. "What?"

"It's a thing with Usher. Some people with my type gradually lose their eyesight as they get older. Balance is another thing that can get wonky. There's no predicting it, and it might not even happen, but it could. Only time will tell."

"Shit."

"Yeah. Shit," I said. "Just another reason we're not a matched set like those two." I inclined my head toward the newlyweds on the dance floor.

"What does that have to do with us being a good match?"

I shook my head in frustration, like he hadn't seen the giant billboard with the flashing lights.

"Are you really ready to be with a deaf *and* blind guy? Do you even understand what that would be like? And if I lost my balance—"

"You don't know what it would be like," he said.

"What?"

"You said I didn't know what that would be like. Well, you don't either. You've never been deaf and blind. I mean, it sounds like shit, but couples deal with shit. It's what they do, right?"

"Ty, we're not talking about a wrecked car or one of us losing a job. I wouldn't be able to take care of myself. I'd lose all my independence and—"

Something clicked in his eyes. I saw it. I couldn't decide if what was coming was good or bad.

"Gabe," he signed my name. "I owe you an answer."

My brow creased again. "What was the question?"

"It's what Lucas asked me over and over. It's the question I dodged like it was a bullet trying to kill me, and it was the most important question he could've asked me."

I didn't even realize I was holding my breath. All the chatter and clatter of the reception faded away. Sam and Miguel vanished. Even the cute little cake toppers disappeared.

All I saw were emerald orbs sparkling as they willed themselves into me.

"The answer is yes."

I felt my eyes moisten. Dammit, I'd made it through the wedding without crying. I would not cry now. Not for this. Definitely not for Tyler.

"I love you, Gabe. I couldn't see through my own stubborn stupidity at the time, but I loved you when Lucas asked me—and I still love you. God, I love you so much it hurts.

"I don't know how to handle you being deaf right now. I don't know what it's like or what it feels like, if you're lonely or just feel alone. I don't know, alright? But I want to. I want to know. I want to learn, and I'm willing to learn.

"If you lose your sight, fuck, I wouldn't know where to start. I can't even imagine . . . I don't want to imagine that. But if it happened, I would do exactly what I'm doing right now. I would learn and grow and make dumb mistakes. I would try and try, and keep trying until something worked.

"I get it if you don't want me back, if I'm too big of a risk—or whatever—because I have *always* been too big of a risk. That's no lie. But I need you to know that my eyes are open and clear, finally.

"I don't want another party or any other man. I want *you*—and Audie—she's part of the package or Dom will kill me. That's all I want. Please."

"I hate you," I said through tears. "I hate you so much."

"I know, but can you hate me a little closer?"

And dammit, my chair slid forward and I felt myself fall into his arms. He held me close against him, like a drowning man clinging to a piece of driftwood, then he buried his face in my neck and began to sob.

I don't know how long we sat there, holding each other and crying, but a firm hand on my shoulder brought me back to the present. I turned to find Miguel with Sam standing behind him. Someone had apparently given them a moist towel because there was no sign of the cake fight from earlier.

"Are you two okay? I guess it's normal to cry at weddings, but isn't this a bit much?"

"Can you married folk fuck off, please? We're having a tender moment over here."

Tyler's muffled voice vibrated past me. I couldn't see his lips, but Miguel and Sam's sudden laughter told me he'd made some smart-ass remark.

"We're okay," I said.

Sam raised a brow.

"Really, we're good."

Chapter 33

TYLER

I t hadn't been easy, those following weeks. Gabe was cautious, and I was sure whispering birds kept his ears full of wisdom and advice. I couldn't blame them. They hadn't been wrong—about me or the challenges we could face in the future.

But they had been wrong about us. I was more certain of that than anything in my life, and I was determined not to screw it up.

Wedding bells were replaced by jingle bells as the holidays consumed everything in sight. Despite winter's chill, Gabe and I bundled up and resumed our evening trips to the dog park. Dom and Audie loved the cold weather and never missed a beat, greeting each other with licks and romps the moment they were freed from the double entrance. It was good to see them back together.

Ben joined us several times a week. It was good for him to have Gabe, another big brother who was also deaf. Watching them interact made me realize how important that sense of community, of commonality, was for both of them. Ben was a great kid, but he'd folded into himself. I was trying to pry him open, but our inability to communicate freely hindered that effort. Gabe slid right between us and bridged the gap.

We spent Sundays with Sam and Miguel, but the tradition evolved into a rotating pattern where they came to my condo every other week so I could cook for the group. I sensed Gabe's hand behind that committee decision, but could never get a straight answer out of the boy, only a request for more lavender ice cream.

Winter drifted to sleep as spring awoke, and we celebrated Gabe's twenty-eighth birthday. At his request, we hosted a small gathering at my condo on the theory Lucas and his posse would be better behaved on our turf. Magically, it worked, and a tenuous peace was formed. I wouldn't say they accepted me, but I took the shift from overt hatred as a positive step.

Our plane swooped low over the crystal sea to land at an airport just inside the coast. The sky was clear, and bright sunlight cast a yellow glow against the ancient stones that overlooked the water. Gabe pointed to one mountain, then another, barely able to keep his focus on one thing at a time. We'd known each other nearly a year, and I'd never seen him so excited.

"I can't believe we're doing this." He practically vibrated. "It's been three years since I've seen my parents and Emilio."

"Then you're long overdue, babe. I'm just glad we're doing it together."

"Me too. You're going to love them, and my mom will eat you alive. Get ready to let those pants out. She will stuff you past your limit. You've been warned."

We gathered our luggage, picked up our rental, and headed toward the edge of the city where Gabe's family lived. Busy streets were quickly re-placed by single-lane roads surrounded by the lush mountain base. We finally pulled into a long gravel driveway. A picket fence surrounded rolling hills covered in thick grass. Two long-legged dogs with mostly white fur and splotches of tan raced to greet us as we stopped before a bright mustard, two-story stucco house that looked older than the United States.

A short woman with graying hair tied in a tight bun emerged, and Gabe couldn't get the car door open fast enough. By the time I reached the front step of the house, Gabe and his mother had been joined by a slim man with black hair, and the trio had devolved into fits of hugs and tears. They prattled in Italian, oblivious to the fact Gabe couldn't hear a word. I'm not sure they registered that I was even standing there watching.

The scene repeated itself a moment later when a twenty-year-old with foppish hair brushed their parents aside and lifted Gabe off the ground.

When the hugs fell away, I watched in wonder as Gabe bounced between the three of them, each speaking rapid Italian, all at the same time. Somehow, he never missed a beat, responding to each with a handful of clipped phrases, before moving to the next.

The babbling suddenly ceased, and four pairs of eyes focused on me.

The dogs barked, and wind rustled the leaves of nearby trees, but no one spoke.

They just stared.

I wanted to crawl under the car.

Then Gabe's mother bounded down the stairs and bowled into me, wrapping her arms around my waist and burying her face in my chest. Before I could react, his dad slammed into my other side, making a Tyler Italiano—or maybe an Ityliano? I wasn't sure what to name that sandwich.

Needless to say, the welcome was warm. Even Gabe's brother stepped down and took my hand, then pulled me in for a half-hug.

Greetings complete, Mom rattled off more Italian, and the men jumped into action. Gabe's dad followed his mom inside, while he and his brother turned toward the car.

"She said dinner will be ready in about thirty minutes, and for us to get our things and get settled. My room's already made and waiting for us."

The idea of us sharing a room under his parents' roof surprised me. My dad would never allow two men to sleep together. We weren't a terribly religious family, but conservative roots ran deep back home. Gabe's folks didn't even blink at the idea.

When dinner hit the table—or began hitting the table—I realized how accurate Gabe's warning had been. Bowls of pasta and platters of fish landed one after the other. I could barely keep up. And there was no chance I would get to make my own plate. Gabe's mom hovered. If even an inch of white ceramic showed for half a second, she scooped and dumped before I could ask what was in the ladle. By my second plate, I wanted to waddle away from the table and take a nap.

My dear Gabe barely slowed as the food kept coming, showering his mother with praise for each dish. She ate it up, giggling in nearly the same way he did when he got tickled.

We fell into an odd rhythm, with one of us speaking, then Gabe translating, then the other responding, and Gabe translating again. I felt bad for him because each time we wanted to chat, he had to stop eating and perform his duties, but he didn't seem to mind.

A few times, he reached over and rubbed my leg or squeezed my hand. I glanced around self-consciously to find Mr. or Mrs. Rossi smiling broadly at their son's affection. There was an unfettered warmth in that home I had never experienced. No one carried on airs or pretense. There was no status or judgment. Only love.

By the time Mrs. Rossi released us from the table, I was stuffed, bordering on miserable. Gabe picked the leftovers off my plate and popped them in his mouth as we stepped away.

"Where do you put it?" I asked as we headed to our room.

He giggled and kissed my cheek.

The next few days ran together. We didn't really do anything, yet we did everything. The Rossis showed us Genoa with the pride of native children. Mr. Rossi told stories of the lands and buildings, while Mrs. Rossi, fascinated by my culinary schooling, spent most of her time talking about ingredients native to the land and cooking techniques. I could've stayed in her kitchen for a year and never learned enough. The woman was a culinary treasure.

On our fifth evening, dinner was a muted affair, at least compared to the previous feasts. Our appetites well sated, we sat around the patio table drinking local wine and enjoying the beauty of the mountains.

Gabe eyed me as I ran my finger around the rim of my wine glass.

"You okay?"

I nodded, but didn't speak. He scrunched up his nose, sensing something amiss.

"I need you to translate for me," I said, steeling my nerves.

He nodded. "Okay. Like I haven't been all week?"

"Just . . . please."

He shrugged.

"Mr. and Mrs. Rossi," I began. "I can't tell you what this week has meant to me . . . to us. Gabe has told me so much about you. He's missed you so much."

I waited for him to translate and for Mrs. Rossi to wipe a tear. She was a crier.

"Before we go, I . . . I need to ask you something."

Gabe hesitated, then translated.

Mr. Rossi leaned in.

"As I understand it, there is a tradition in Italy. I've never been a religious man, but I have great respect for customs. Culinary school instilled that in me."

Mrs. Rossi smiled broadly at that.

"You see, I've never . . . I mean, when I met . . . I'm sorry."

Gabe stopped translating and cocked his head.

"I'm okay. Come on," I said to him.

"Mr. Rossi, I've known a lot of people, but I've never met anyone like Gabe. There's something truly special and unique about him. I knew it the first time we met, and I've been trying to identify it ever since."

Gabe's translation was halting as he struggled to translate what felt like highly personal compliments.

Mrs. Rossi reached over and took her husband's hand.

"Until I came here, I didn't truly understand, but I do now. I've watched Gabe's kindness. I've seen his compassion and warmth. I feel his laughter every day, and could never get enough of his smile. Each of those are pieces of the spirit I've felt here, with you. This place, this family, it is warmth, and life, and soul. It is beauty and peace. It is love."

I glanced at Gabe as he spoke. His lower lip was quivering.

"Mr. and Mrs. Rossi, I had to learn some tough lessons this past year, mostly about myself, who I wanted to be, things like that. The most important thing I learned, though, was about Gabe.

"I learned he is the most amazing man I have ever known. I learned he lifts my heart when it isn't strong enough to face the day. I learned his joy is infectious, and that it heals. Most importantly, I learned I don't want to live a single day without him in my life, no matter what that life may bring.

"Mr. and Mrs. Rossi, I want to marry your son. Please. May I have your blessing?"

Gabe choked out the last words as Mrs. Rossi completely fell apart.

Mr. Rossi rose and closed the distance between us, then wrapped me in his arms and kissed my cheek.

I didn't need a translation for the words he whispered.

"*Sì, figlio mio, sì.*"

Dearest Reader,

Thank you for joining me on the journey of Tyler and Gabe. If you loved ***I Hear You***, please take a moment to leave a review filled with stars. Your feedback inspires authors to create more stories.

Casey

Reference

According to the U.S. National Institute on Deafness and Other Communications Disorders, a division of the U.S. Department of Health, Usher syndrome is the most common condition that affects both hearing and vision; sometimes it also affects balance.

Deafness or hearing loss in Usher syndrome is caused by abnormal development of hair cells (sound receptor cells) in the inner ear. Most children with Usher syndrome are born with moderate to profound hearing loss, depending on the type. Less commonly, hearing loss from Usher syndrome appears during adolescence or later. Usher syndrome can also cause severe balance problems due to abnormal development of the vestibular hair cells, sensory cells that detect gravity and head movement.

Books by Casey Morales

Nashville Spicy series

Raised by Wolves series

About Your Author

Casey Morales is an LGBT storyteller and the author of multiple bestselling MM romance novels. Born in the Southern United States, Casey is an avid tennis player, aspiring chef, dog lover, and ravenous consumer of gummy bears.

www.ingramcontent.com/pod-product-compliance
Lightning Source LLC
Chambersburg PA
CBHW060902210726

48293CB00006B/1927